All the best!

Table 21

T. Rafael Cimino

Akula Media Group and BMG Publishing
Akula Media Group, Inc., 7408 Coastal Way, Huntersville, North Carolina, USA 28078. BMG Publishing, a BMG Company. (310) 890-5485

Published simultaneously in Canada and Europe.

Library of Congress Cataloging-in-Publication Data
T. Rafael Cimino
Table 21 / T. Rafael Cimino

ISBN-13: 978-0-615-48443-3
ISBN-10: 0-615-48443-3

1. Crime-Fiction 2. Thriller-Fiction 3. Drama-Fiction

Printed in the United States of America.
1 2 3 4 5 6 7 8 9

Cover design by Janelle Young and the Author.
Senior Editor: Joe Statile

Also by T. Rafael Cimino

Mid Ocean

Rivertown

Please Visit

TRCimino.com

For Svetlina and Stephanie.
My family and my heart.

Prologue

February 15, 1974

After a night of falling snow, the morning was clear with a unique stillness and a white blanket that covered every inch of 9th Street in Central Brooklyn. Soft rolling hills in the shapes of the cars the snow had covered lined the street that was marked with tall iron lampposts embedded into the edge of the sidewalk. Shop owners had been out early to clear the portion in front of their respective stores. A baker that was up at 4:30 got a head start while his ovens were warming up. Now the smell of fresh bread filled the air, complementing the already beautiful day.

Traffic on the street had started to flow slowly with each car navigating through the tracks of the one before it. Thick plumes of steam arose from the different tailpipes as the warm air condensed and dripped to the snow below.

Many of the street side shops had been decorated for this day with red hearts and cutouts of flying cupids blowing into long declaring horns or shooting arrows of love and adoration.

On the sidewalk, Bettina Cooper struggled to maintain her footing on the slippery concrete beneath her feet. Normally this sidewalk would be crowded with people, but it was Sunday, and the day after a civil holiday at that. Still, she did the best she could, giving thanks for the clear patches and for those who had shoveled the snow at such an early hour. At eight months pregnant it was hard for her to maintain her balance. The exponential growth of her body above the waistline made her top heavy, requiring her to watch every step. Since she was a nursing student she knew that a fall at this stage of the pregnancy would have been catastrophic. At twenty-five she had finished the academic portion of her nurse's training and was in her second term for the practical portion of her degree. She had been assigned an intensive rotation in the emergency room at the Methodist Hospital of Brooklyn and, after two long years of classroom instruction, was looking forward to getting to finally apply some of what she had learned. Things hadn't been easy for her. While she had earned a full scholarship to the State University of New York at Downstate in Brooklyn, her unplanned pregnancy came close to derailing her plans to graduate and sit for her state nursing boards by her twenty-sixth birthday. Bettina was well liked though and had earned the respect of her professors and clinical instructors, especially Maria Gomez, a hospital nurse preceptor who took Bettina under her wing. While maintaining the set standard, the older nurse cut her some slack where she could. At the end of her last class she had managed to maintain a solid 3.8 grade point average and not miss a single session.

Bettina was an attractive girl. While other black girls her age wore their hair in large afros, she was more conservative. Her black locks hung down in tight curls that bounced off her shoulders. Her face was sculpted with a European influence. High cheekbones rounded down to her full lips and attracted so many. Her eyes were a mysterious green and from them danced delicate brown lashes that resembled a pair of butterflies.

She wished she could have tucked her hands into the front of her silk-lined jacket but it took both hands to carry the stack of books she needed for the different segments of her training. Underneath the jacket she wore her bright white student nurse's uniform and on her head, a heavily starched white nurse's cap.

The day before had changed her life. She met her boyfriend, the father of her baby, for a quiet Valentine's dinner in his apartment followed by a night of warm cohesiveness. Their relationship had, before this day, been clandestine but at 4:00 AM she awoke to find an engagement ring in a small box on the pillow next to her. She had been waking at all hours of the night to readjust her growing body. This one time though, she rolled towards his side. Perplexed, she couldn't help but notice the felt covered gray box atop his pillow. It had been wrapped in a red ribbon. The ring had belonged to his grandmother and was unusual in that the center-mounted diamond of a carat and a half was joined on either side by two brilliant green emeralds.

As Bettina continued to walk on the snow-covered sidewalk, she twisted her right thumb towards her ring finger. She had to feel it again. The touch of the ring alone put a smile on her face. It would have been a romantic gesture on any occasion, but it was made more special since it was yesterday, Valentine's Day, the holiest of days for young lovers and those that wanted to be both young and in love.

Because of the street traffic, she never noticed the unmarked police cruiser that lumbered behind her. The 1972 Plymouth Fury was painted white and blended in to the landscape. It moved so slowly that without the rising steam from the exhaust pipe, one would have thought it wasn't running at all.

From inside the Plymouth, two detectives from the NYPD Organized Crime Unit watched and waited. The chatter of a squawking police radio competed with the constant drone of the car's heater.

Bettina looked down at her simple Timex watch that told her she was running late. She had despised shortcuts but she was cold and her shoes were wet. The young woman had, after all, traveled this way almost everyday to the hospital but that failed to alleviate her feelings of discomfort. The alley she entered sliced in between a meat packing plant and an abandoned warehouse and the route saved her three full blocks.

Inside the car, the two detectives looked at each other with concern. "What the hell is she doing?" Detective Stanley Fitzgerald asked. "Fitz," as he was known by the other officers in his precinct, was a five year veteran of the NYPD and had been with the Organized Crime Unit for a little over eight months, becoming the first black officer to enter the elite and exclusive squad.

"She's cutting over to 8th," answered Bill Stewart, Fitz's partner. Stewart had twin boys that were getting ready to graduate from college. He had been with the NYPD right out of high school and had worked his way up the ranks, securing a sergeant's rate ten years before. Fitz looked up to his partner and tried to follow his lead whenever he could. Most in the unit did.

"I don't like this," Fitz objected.

Bettina was pleased that the snow had been partially diverted by an overhang four stories above. She walked faster as she kept her focus on the well-lit opening at the other end of the alley just five hundred feet away. Still, she felt uncomfortable. The city had its dark places and this was one of them. The air had grown colder as the tall buildings on either side shielded the rising sun. Without a constant breeze, the stench of garbage was stagnant. It was much quieter here. She could hear the ice and snow crunch beneath her wet feet. Garbage had been piled up along the brick walls. Discarded wrapping paper and other heart-shaped decorations were a reminder that the romantic holiday was over. It was time for people to get back to life as they knew it.

She looked up at the suspended icicles hanging from the different fire escapes and realized she was almost halfway through. Bettina started to walk faster and that's when it happened. Without warning, a trashcan turned over with the echoing sound of hollow tin hitting bare concrete. She jumped and turned towards the sound just in time to see an overgrown Siamese cat scurry away from her. As she turned to resume her walk, Bettina came face to face with him. He wasn't much taller than she was and wore a black jacket, a gray pair of jogging pants, tennis shoes and a blue and white ski mask.

"Please, don't hurt me. I have to get to work. They are waiting for me," she pleaded as the man looked at her in silence. Then, like it was his first time, the man tried to pull from what she could see was a gun from his jacket. In his haste, the hammer of the small caliber pistol got caught within the cloth lining of his jacket pocket. Seeing her opportunity, Bettina dropped her books and ran for the opening, now just a few hundred feet away. The man took both hands and untangled the gun from his pocket as he took aim at the fleeing girl. As the gun fired, the loud percussion broke the ice and snow free from the surrounding buildings and a small pod of pigeons burst out over the main street.

The white Plymouth Fury pulled up against the exiting side of the alley. Despite the radio and the heater, the two policemen heard the shot as it echoed from between the buildings. Fitz was the first one out of the car with his snub-nosed .38 in hand. Bill was a car length behind him. The two were a hundred feet into the alley before they saw her, the dark outline of her body and the unborn mound that made up her abdomen. She was seizing violently from the single shot to the back of her head. Fitz got down on one knee and tried to stomach the sight of the girl's disfigured face as he called into his portable radio.

"Alpha 36, Alpha 36...we need an EMU to that alley at..." Fitz paused as he stood to look around and get his bearings. That's when he saw the gun. In an instant, he dove to the hard ground as another shot rang out. Fitz pointed in the general direction down the alley and unloaded the six rounds from his small revolver as he heard the sound of fleeing footsteps. And then it was silent.

"Alpha 36?" the radio squawked.

"Bill?" Fitz called out, turning around to see his partner lying motionless on the alley floor in a pool of his own blood. Sergeant Bill Stewart had a wife and two sons. He had been a twenty-one year veteran of the NYPD and was now lying motionless on the cold, dark floor of the alley with a sizable hole in his head. Fitz fought to control his breathing.

"Alpha 36 – Alpha 36! Officer down!" he yelled.

"Location Alpha 36?"

"Back alley…behind…back alley," he cried out of breath. "Two victims! Send EMU!"

"Location Alpha 36?"

"Back alley…9th and Byrne."

Chapter 1

Thanksgiving 1999

The sprawling Staten Island estate of Ray Sabarese Senior occupied three full well landscaped acres. In the center, protected by wrought iron gates, fifty surveillance cameras and three armed guards sat the main residence, thirteen thousand feet of handcrafted architecture, trimmed in marble, granite and as much ornate opulence as their money could buy.

As a soft snow fell outside, his family sat warm and content along both sides of a long oak table with Ray Senior at one end and his youngest son, Roman Sabarese at the other. On one side and sitting next to the patriarch was his invalid wife Lucia, who sat in a state of stupor confined to a clumsy wheelchair. Across from her was Max Weintraub, the family's lawyer. Nello Falcone and his wife Marjory occupied seats adjacent to Roman and across from them sat an empty chair that stayed reserved, year after year, for the oldest Sabarese son, Ray Junior, who passed away seven years before, the victim of a drug overdose.

This was Lucia's favorite season of the year and Thanksgiving was her favorite day. Despite the full staff of servants, including a chef, two maids and a houseboy, she had always insisted on preparing the annual meal herself. Italian Thanksgiving meals were different than those of traditional Americans. Pork, pasta and the three rich gravies, red, pomadore, and alfredo, replaced the American turkey, dressing and cranberry sauce. This was, after all, about family and what better way to connect to the old country than to dust off the classic recipes that had been prepared for generations. For Lucia, this had been the one meal she prepared herself, planning the menu a month ahead of time, going to the farmer's market and making every strand of pasta in her kitchen. For this event, she was the artist and the Thanksgiving table was her canvas.

Only a decade later and it was all she could do to hold up her own head as she sat in a semi-vegetative state. She had been diagnosed with an extreme case of Alzheimer's disease shortly after Ray Junior's death. As everyone else talked and got comfortable, she just stared. A small thread of drool lapsed through the corner of her drooping mouth as her loving Ray Senior reached over with a napkin to blot it.

As the house staff brought out the food, Ray Senior cataloged each dish as though he was announcing a football game.

"Hey, look what we got here. Some buffalo mozzarella with the biggest tomatoes in all of the north," he continued with vigor towards his wife, "look at this Momma."

"Looks good," Nello said with a smile.

"Hey, I hope we got some kosher stuff for Maxi here," Ray Senior said, looking over his shoulder at one of the maids.

This was to be Max's first Thanksgiving with his employers. He had entered a difficult divorce a year before and, at the urging of Ray Senior, decided to spend the holiday amongst friends.

"Don't worry about it Senior. I don't really practice…" Max replied.

"That's right, you ain't a kosher Jew. I forgot. Well, you're all in for a treat," he continued.

As the last dish, a steaming plate of pork sausage and peppers, was carried into the dining room, the second maid entered behind with a concerned look on her face.

"Mister Ray! Mister Ray! The TV no work," the Venezuelan announced.

"What the hell is she talking about?" Ray Senior asked as he motioned to his son at the other end of the table.

Outside the compound four black Chevrolet Suburbans pulled up to the gate as two more drove down a side street, depositing their occupants around the rear of the estate. Back at the front, a single man clad in the standard Kevlar helmet vest and with an MP-3 fully automatic machine gun slung over his shoulder, disabled the armature to the front iron gate with a pair of oversized bolt cutters. With a *SNAP* the tool sheered the linkage that secured the sliding gate. A second later, the man rolled it open and the four-car detail rolled into a large circular drive that rounded a flowing fountain and an immaculately manicured lawn.

Back inside the dining room, Roman tried to make sense of what was happening.

"Rosa. What TV?" he asked.

"The 'curity TV is no working. Is snow. Blanco," she stammered with her best spanglish as Roman stood and walked into the kitchen with the maid on his heels.

"See. No TV," she repeated, pointing to the wall-mounted monitors for the house's elaborate camera surveillance system.

"It must be a fluke," he reasoned, returning to the dining room.

"What is it Roman?" Ray Senior asked as his son made his way over to a widow.

"Cameras are out and we've got some movement on the back lawn."

"Damn Russians!" Ray Senior yelled, throwing his napkin on the table before standing.

"Nello, go to the front," Roman ordered. "You got a piece?"

"It's in the car," Nello replied.

"Just as well. I think these guys are cops," Roman advised.

"Cops?" Ray Senior blurted out. "Are you crazy son? On Thanksgiving?"

Then without warning, a solid impact struck the front door's handle mechanism sending pieces of the lock scattering across the marble floor of the foyer. As the door swung open, Nello and Roman rushed in to see a wide-open space where the door was closed a few seconds before. The black armored suits of the intruders entered next with guns drawn and the lead man looked Roman square in the face.

"FBI! Freeze! We have multiple warrants!"

"Nello…get Max!" Roman yelled as his friend headed towards the kitchen.

"I said freeze!" the man repeated as Nello stopped mid-step with his hands raised over his head.

A crash sounded a few seconds later from deeper inside the residence as the rear detail crashed through a backset of glass-paned French doors.

"What is the meaning of this?" Ray Senior yelled.

"Rafael Peter Sabarese?" another agent asked. "We have a federal warrant for your arrest."

"Max! Do something!" he pleaded.

"Ray, I'm a tax attorney," Max whispered up to his standing boss who was shouting with his mouth half full of food. "Ask them for a copy of the warrant."

"You ask them!" his boss redirected.

"Agent," Max said, standing in front of the table. "Can I see the warrant please?"

"I thought you'd never ask," the lead agent answered, walking into the dining room with Nello and Roman in handcuffs. "Here you go."

"Jesus!" Max said as he accepted the one hundred and forty-seven page document.

"I'll save you some time counselor. There's two hundred and eleven felony counts there, a seizure order for the house and all its contents, including the six cars in the different garages and an order to search the said premises."

"And them?" Max said, pointing to Nello and Roman.

"Oh, they're free to go as soon as we're done."

"Thank God," Nello's wife sighed as she motioned the four points of a cross on her chest.

"The next time you disobey the order of a federal officer, you could get shot," the agent said to Nello as the sound of a circling helicopter filled the room.

In time, two dozen more agents entered and started digging through every cabinet, closet and dresser drawer. Lucia was wheeled to the center of the room where she sat with a small tear that continued to run down her wrinkled face. Ray Sabarese Senior was led out of the house in handcuffs as scores of curious neighbors looked on from the winding sidewalks that ran around the compound.

Within the hour Senior was booked into federal custody at the Federal Processing Center in Danbury, Connecticut. While he had planned to retire to bed early with a full stomach and a glass of brandy, Ray Sabarese Senior was now wearing an orange jumpsuit and his bed would consist of a three-inch mat that covered a rusty steel meshed frame. During his arraignment a few days later, and despite the numerous pleas from a seasoned criminal defense attorney, bail was denied. Senior had been part of a statewide sweep that netted the government over a hundred arrests and the confiscation of assets worth two hundred million dollars.

Chapter 2

December 27th
Monday, 9:15 PM
98 hours, 45 minutes left

It looked like any other courtroom. Sixteen-foot-high cherry wood veneer walls rose from the commercially carpeted floors to the white architectural ceilings that were overhead. Like many other courtrooms, the judge's bench sat high in the front center of the room that looked more like a church than a staple of justice. To the right of the judge's bench, a young black woman sat in the witness box. Her finely tuned body language was in defensive mode. Shay Jefferson was on trial for negligent homicide, implicated in the deaths of her two young children after she left them alone and their apartment caught fire.

To the left, a court reporter typed away as the prosecutor hammered the defendant with a set of probing questions.

"Are you trying to tell this court that your children were safe in bed and under the watchful eye of a fully qualified sitter when you left your apartment?" Chelsea Waters, the young idealistic prosecutor asked.

"Yes ma'am," the witness answered with a trembling voice.

"I'll add, you left your apartment to meet your boyfriend at Happy's Bar and Grill on 23rd and 5th," Waters continued.

"I said they was, didn't I?" she replied, more defensively this time.

"So how is it Miss Jefferson that your two children, Terrence and Shanika, ended up dead, suffocated in their sleep by smoke from a fire; a fire that started from a space heater in your apartment?"

"I was jus tryin' to keep 'em warm…"

"Oh they got warm alright…"

"Please stop! We jus po' and from tha ghetto. Ain't got nothin'."

"It's no excuse Miss Jefferson. I know what it's like to be cold and on your own."

"You ain't black like me. You an oreo and a half-breed at that!" she finished with spirit, referencing the prosecutor's mixed race.

Unlike other courtrooms, the judge didn't interfere with the drama that was unfolding. And unlike other courtrooms, Tim Bussy, a bearded television director, stood off to one side of the room wearing headphones as the cameras rolled simultaneously. This was a complex New Jersey soundstage and beyond the cherry wood pews and judge's bench, rows of black directional stage lights hung from the steel rafters of the immense building's ceiling. On the floor, far from the camera's view, various wires covered the concrete, some taped in place by union gaffers, some an inch thick.

"Cut!" the director yelled. "That's much better. Let's wrap for the long week. The next time we meet it will be in the new millennium."

The courtroom's spectators, paid extras, and the rest of the cast cleared the elaborate set. As they exited to different parts of the building, Zoë Greene, who played Chelsea Waters, walked over to the director.

"So, did you get a chance to look at my script?" she asked.

"I did, and it's been sent upstairs. Good stuff Zoë."

"Thanks."

"I can't make any promises, you understand," the director added.

"Of course. I just had some ideas."

"And some good ones. I'll see what I can do."

"Thanks Tim."

"So what do you think of this?" the director asked, pointing to the set. "Too ghetto?"

"Yeah, just a bit," she replied honestly.

"The problem is the public thinks this shit is real."

"And that's how perception becomes reality," Zoë replied as the director smiled with enlightened eyebrows.

"So what's the plan after we wrap the season?" he asked.

"I've been offered a supporting role in an urban piece."

"Urban?"

"You know, all black cast. I think I'm the only member with a last name, the token chestnut."

"You going to take it?"

"Haven't decided yet."

The Prosecutor was a new cable favorite and was enjoying higher than normal ratings for its second season. The show and its Sunday night timeslot were the perfect springboard for A-lister Zoë Greene, a blossoming young actress and recent graduate of NYU's film school.

The premise of the show was simple. The lead role, Gloria, was a tough street-smart African American woman who worked her way up from the streets to become a leading New York prosecutor. Her protégé, Chelsea Waters, grew up in an apartment on Park Avenue and was a recent graduate of Yale Law. Each week another case unfolded on the television sets of millions of Americans as the two lawyers fought crime and, on more than one occasion, each other.

After giving her director a departing hug, Zoë walked over and joined the other cast members at the craft services table.

"So what are your plans for the big holiday?" Emily Butters, the actress who played Shay Jefferson asked.

"I've got to do some live countdown show for NBC. Besides that, I'm free," Zoë replied as she grabbed a plastic bottle of Evian mineral water.

"Some friends and I are doing a rooftop thing in the Village. You're welcome to join."

"I might take you up on that. I promised my mom we'd spend some time together, but she's likely to be in bed by ten or so. I'll call you."

"Great job by the way," Butters said, pointing to the courtroom set.

"You too," Zoë replied with a smile and soft hand on her fellow actress's shoulder.

In real life Zoë grew up in Brooklyn, the half black daughter of a white single mother. She had paid her dues, working her way through college after graduating from the Children's Professional High School in Manhattan. Once in the NYU film program, she excelled while working nights at a restaurant in Tribeca. Her mother became involved in her career and pushed her to attend casting calls and screen tests where her face became a regular between the different agencies. She persevered and grew. Then a chance meeting between Zoë and one of *The Prosecutor's* producers changed her life. He had been giving a talk for one of her classes and she was the one asking all the questions. Before the class was over, the producer had made a mental note to give the budding actress a screen test and within a week, the role of Chelsea Waters was filled. Zoë graduated that May and started shooting the pilot the next month. When attentive audiences watched the first show in September, it was an instant hit, capturing the lion's share of the Neilsen ratings and placing third behind NBC's *ER* and *Seinfeld,* both of which had shares in the low twenties. *The Prosecutor* wasn't far behind with a solid seventeen.

Now she was off for ten days. Her seventy-hour weeks were starting to catch up with her metabolism, which was kept alive with coffee, Diet Coke and her favorite energy drink of the month. Zoë made her way out of the building and in to a rented blue Chevrolet Corvette that sat parked in her reserved parking space, a few of the perks of the business. A few minutes later and she was headed towards the city for dinner with friends at the one place she knew better than most, the restaurant where she had worked her way through college.

Chapter 3

11:07 PM
96 hours, 53 minutes left

The length of Greenwich Street between Chambers and Harrison was illuminated by a series of streetlights that sat perched atop matching iron lampposts that were spaced every hundred feet. On the west side of the street, a tall iron fence separated the sidewalk from the expanse of the three acre Washington Market Park, a local retreat for three generations of New Yorkers and a place where families could enjoy the outdoors in a city known for its concrete, brick and mortar. The other side of Greenwich was occupied by a long string of local businesses. Most of the space was occupied with art galleries, haberdasheries, two bakeries, a deli and one lone restaurant that sat in the center of the building. While most of the shops were closed, Evangeline's was busier than normal This was after all, as the *Times* called it, "the hottest Italian restaurant and one of the oldest in the Tribeca district of Manhattan."

It was a Monday and, while a slow night for other restaurants, Evangeline's was averaging a ninety-minute wait time for a decent table. Regardless, with less than five days left in the expiring millennium, the patrons of Evangeline's were in the mood to celebrate. They were at the precipice. The promise of a new age was littered with the apprehension of the unknown where the religious zealots were having a field day. Vague predictions combined with a feeling of ambivalence by those who feared the future and the change it could bring set the stage for an undertone of repressed hysteria. On a more legitimate scale, computer experts worldwide warned of a systematic shutdown at the stroke of midnight that would affect everything from electrical power grids to missile defense systems. Still, most of the population didn't take any of these premonitions too seriously. For them, this was going to be the party of a lifetime.

Evangeline's fifty-five year old general manager Nello Falcone leaned his heavy frame against the bar as he oversaw his staff tend to the customers, wondering for the umpteenth time that day when it would all end.

"Devon, bus table three. Let's go!" he ordered as he spied Devon Sandles, the restaurant's forty-two year old dishwasher taking an extra break inside the kitchen. Devon, who had been with Evangeline's since his teen years, had shared his life with a serious case of Down syndrome. He was part of the Evangeline's family though, and that meant he had the love and respect of the rest of the staff.

While Nello wasn't a religious man, he did, out of the corner of his left ear, pay attention to the crazy predictions being repeated around him, especially those of the sixteenth century astronomer Michel Nostradamus who had been featured almost daily on the local PBS channel. *Was this going to be the end of civilization as we know it?* he had asked himself. The crowd was certainly tweaked higher than normal. His staff of bartenders and line cooks bragged about how much easier it was to get laid now that the local women were thinking in terms of time and opportunity. If nothing else, the uncertainty of it all made for an interesting pick-up line.

To add to the chaos, America was at war with Islam and itself. Six years before, the World Trade Center was the subject of a terrorist bombing. Two years later the Alfred P. Murrah Federal Building had been decimated in Oklahoma City killing one hundred and sixty-eight people, including nineteen preschool children that were in the building's daycare center. And to top it off, the U.S. President had been impeached, the only one in U. S. history with the exception of Andrew Johnson. This reminded everyone that in this day and age, *anything* was possible.

Everything was running smoothly, which was not always the case. On a night like this, one mistake could set the ticket times back twenty minutes; twenty minutes could cost ten thousand dollars or more. Nello was usually ahead of any critical issues. He had been with the Sabarese family since the restaurant opened in June of 1963 and had been a loyal captain.

"Hey Nello!" a voice said, breaking the floor manager's concentration.

"Zoë!" he replied giving her a tight hug. "How was your last day of shooting?"

"Great. They're considering a script I wrote for the next season. I'm so excited!"

"I always knew this acting this was a stepping stone for you," Nello said.

"Thanks Nello…it means a lot," she said as she walked towards Roman.

Nello thought back to the first day he met her. She was fresh out of high school and looking for a job. She had been accepted to NYU's film school and needed to supplement her student loans and grants with twenty hours a week.

"I need someone that can run the podium. It takes guts and a strong will," he had told her. The memory had put a smile on his face. One of the many kids he had seen come and go through the years, although not many made of themselves what Zoë had. Still, the idea of being a mentor to so many was a comfort to him. This was, after all, his extended family and with that he gladly welcomed all the responsibilities that came his way.

"My mom says I'm pretty strong willed," she had replied.

"But can you take orders? I don't have time for no teenager bullshit," he had told her.

"Yes sir, I can. I will be here whenever you need me, especially the weekends," she stressed, immediately impressing him.

"Don't you want to go out and party with your friends?"

"I don't go out much. I only go to the movies and then only on Tuesday nights because it's half price."

"Hey boss!" a voice rang out from the present, breaking his sentimental memory. "The fan motor in the overhead vent is starting to heat up again."

"I'll be right there," Nello answered with a sigh, tossing a fresh rag over his shoulder.

It was a lot of work running any restaurant. It was twice as much running a successful one. Seven days a week the staff came in early full of energy and left late, depleted and tired. And Nello had seen it all from the first day they opened the place.

It had been thirty-six years ago and the event captured the entire community that summer day in June of 1963 when Ray Sabarese Senior, known on the street as "Senior," started the restaurant then called *La Trattoria*. The police had shut down both ends of Greenwich Street for the day as a new era had been born. For the kids that played across the street at the Washington Market Park, Ray Senior himself served free cups of frozen gelato and with that small gesture of kindness, the Tribeca community accepted the bistro of forty-five tables as an instant landmark. The Sabareses welcomed all their associates, wise guys in the front, cops and city officials in the back. They were all cops and crooks, neither and both.

As far as the books were concerned, La Trattoria was a huge success. The restaurant didn't actually do a lot business though. It was more of a clubhouse; a place guys could go and be guys, tell bad jokes, reminisce about the good ole' days and get away from the rigors of domestic life. Back then the place was closed on Sundays. Senior would say, "you can hide from the law, you can hide from your wives, but you can't hide from God." But the other six days a week the kitchen turned out the most aromatic blends of sausage and peppers, linguini with clam sauce, baked ziti and the house specialty, capellini sirenetta, which was a dish of angel hair pasta with shrimp and arugula in a light tomato sauce.

At the end of 1965, a U.S. Senator from New York, in conjunction with the Italian Embassy in Washington, arranged for La Trattoria to be declared an official annex of Italy's New York Consulate Office. This diplomatic status gave Senior the ability to operate from the restaurant without the fear of search, seizure or wiretaps. For four years the restaurant ran like a Swiss clock. And then, on the eve Senior's second and youngest son Roman returned from the Vietnam War, a federal indictment was handed down accusing thirty-four of the establishment's regulars with charges ranging from racketeering and loan sharking to extortion and money laundering. Senior was untouched, but many within his organization took the fall for the rest. Unfortunately for the family, many of the accused turned state's evidence and implicated a series of New York's finest along with a handful of city councilmen, the Tribeca president, the deputy mayor and the fire department's head of inspections. In the end, fifty-four men were arrested and charged in the largest organized crime sweep of its time. As a result, a huge divide was instituted between the Sabareses and the police. Resentment became so great that cops walking the beat would go across Greenwich Street to avoid being seen in front of the restaurant.

In a defensive move, the family circled the wagons. The restaurant, after all, was protected like the Vatican itself. La Trattoria became a city within a city. Senior immediately developed a low profile, placing Roman in charge of the restaurant.

Roman Sabarese was affiliated with the family because he was born into it. He had been a stellar student, a decorated war veteran and the successful owner of the renamed Evangeline's for over twenty-six years, a millennium of its own in restaurant terms. Roman had a different level of discipline than most and a stronger work ethic. His time in the Army and successes while at war had shaped him into a man of integrity. Despite his victories though, many said his war record didn't count because the Vietnam conflict was illegitimate in nature. "Tell that to the guys we left behind," Roman would say in a reserved, cigar smoking voice.

It was clear from the beginning that Roman was different from the first time his mother Lucia had to visit his school because he'd gotten into trouble. There had been a fight between some gang members and a group of his friends in the schoolyard after class. The youngest Sabarese, at age twelve, had taken a pipe and reduced the older thugs to crying youngsters with bloodstained clothes. In the end, the gang kids were arrested and Roman was hailed as a hero by everyone, a position he soon cherished within himself.

Years later when he was sent to Vietnam, he developed a new respect for his life and an appreciation for those who gave their own. He returned to Manhattan, torn and tattered like an old flag, with a Purple Heart in one hand and a drab green duffle in the other, home to his parents who had tried so hard to keep him close and safe. Unbeknownst to them, he had returned a changed man.

For Roman, the time he invested into the restaurant represented half his life. Every year, the restaurant got a little better, made a larger profit and became, in the process, more refined. The process also had an affect on Roman. Besides his one cigar a day habit, he indulged in few vices. He didn't drink and never partook in drugs. He avoided prescription medications and rarely saw a doctor. He was in bed by midnight and up by six and usually slept alone. Roman Sabarese had one recipient of his life's work: Evangeline's. It was his friend, his wife and his world. The restaurant business consumed him and he disappeared into it, completely overtaken by its rigor and daily demands.

Roman sat quietly at his private table reviewing a spreadsheet with the next day's orders and his current inventory, keeping a corner of an eye reserved for the customers and their respective levels of satisfaction. Regardless of who he was or who he was trying to be, the patrons of Evangeline's came first.

In the kitchen Luigi Vacile ("Gigi" to those who knew him) was a veteran of the better Italian kitchens in the city, having earned his stripes on Little Italy's famed Mulberry Street. Backing him up was Ruhel, his sous chef, an Indian national and a graduate of Apicius, the Culinary Institute of Florence. Ruhel spent his afternoons and nights in the restaurant and his mornings studying his Hindu faith, sending most of his earnings home to his family in Mumbai.

On the floor were some of the busiest waiters in the city. Lisa and Jess, twins from Australia, covered the back balcony, a portion of the restaurant that was elevated a few feet above the rest of the dining room. Their sixteen tables had been reserved for VIPs, locals, and the regular patrons that were usually more generous with their tips. This was a station the girls had worked hard to earn and maintain.

On the ground level were five other waiters, both male and female, who rotated their stations. In the front, two attractive hostesses stood their ground as the guardians of who would get a table and who wouldn't.

Most restaurants numbered their tables and Evangeline's was no exception. Some of the tables though, like real estate, were worth more than others, both more to the patrons and more to those who waited on them. Table 15 on the back balcony was the honeymoon suite of the restaurant. It had been reserved for VIPs and had been the site of almost two hundred proposals over the years. Table 3 was tucked away in a quiet corner and was used by many celebrities who wanted to be anonymous. Table 9 was positioned next to the kitchen door and was assigned to all the new wait staff since those who ate there usually tipped the least. Table 40 had one leg a shave shorter than the rest so it wobbled, table 28 sat under an air vent and dripped condensed water during the warm months, table 34 was so close to the bar that customers could reach behind and have their drinks refilled (and often did), and table 21 belonged to Roman. It was the owner's table, *his* table, and no one sat there but him and his guests. It was the nuances of this place that made it so special and despite the minor issues, the memorable significantly outweighed the forgettable, and that's what kept people coming back in drones.

Across the room, Roman's eyes lit up as Zoë approached 21. She had been working on the set of her show for the last month, investing almost fourteen hours a day, and now she could take a breath and relax.

"Busy night," Zoë remarked as she slid into the round booth.

"I'm glad I decided to close for the weekend," Roman replied, moving over to accommodate his young friend. "Tell me again, what you are doing for the New Year?"

"I've got to do a live show on Friday night for NBC, and you know, plug my show, and then, who knows," she replied with ambivalence. "My mom wants to see me after that, but she'll be in bed by ten or eleven. What are you doing?"

"Ten or eleven sounds pretty good to me right about now."

"You're crazy. It's the biggest New Year we will ever see in our lifetime. The birth of the new millennium."

"Actually, the birth of the new millennium is next year."

"I know, we've had this discussion already, but perception..."

"Perception is reality... I know, I know," Roman interrupted.

"Hey Zoë," Jess, one of the Australian twins said as she approached to take their order. "What are you hungry for?"

"I have had a craving for Luigi's calamari with my special recipe for a couple of days now. It's been driving me crazy," she said with a big smile.

"One special calamari for Zoë," Jess said, turning to her boss. "Roman, you ready for me to put yours in?"

"Sure, and bring me another coffee."

The waitress walked back to the ticket station and yelled back, "portobello steak with angel hair and a special calamari for 21."

"Special calamari?" Ruhel the sous chef called back.

"It's for Zoë."

"Very special then...coming up!"

Chapter 4

Tuesday 1:35 AM
94 hours, 35 minutes left

Tommy Bonatrelli, called *T-bone* by those who knew him - *Bones* by those who knew him better - cruised the streets of Bedford Stuyvesant in his 1986 Ford Bronco. He had waited for this small bit of freedom. At fifty-seven, he had spent the last twelve years and nine months counting the days as he served out his prescribed prison sentence at the Terre Haute Federal Correctional Facility in mid-state Illinois. For him this had been a long time coming. Two days before he had boarded a bus that brought him to Queens, the home of his aged mother and old stomping grounds. When he left New York almost thirteen years before, he did so with the fond farewells of his friends and family who treated him to an all-encompassing departure party complete with good food, potent spirits and a night of arranged affection with the most beautiful girl he had ever seen. That was the last time he saw his friends and felt the tender touch of a woman, precisely why this night's mission was so important.

T-bone cruised the streets slowly. It was dark and his four wheel drive utility vehicle stood out in a sea of over-decorated and resurrected Chevrolet Impalas, Lincoln Mark Vs, and Cadillac Eldorados. The truck had been his last indulgence before going away. He bought it as a gift to himself, something to look forward to when he eventually got out. His friends had joked with him calling the truck a redneck Mercedes. It was, after all, a strange purchase for a man who was part of a culture that admired the finest luxury automobiles. At his departure party, the parking spaces that fronted his favorite restaurant on Greenwich Street were filled with new Mercedes, Town Cars, Porches and standing higher than all the rest with its oversized tires, his new Ford Bronco. It was so new that it still had the window sticker applied to the passenger side window and its interior had the aroma that cost so much to acquire.

T-bone had never been considered an overly smart man to his friends or to himself. He was wise enough though to foresee what his life would be like once he had completed his sentence. Knowing that his twelve plus years would be filled with confinement and the close proximity to hundreds of other inmates, he strategized his post sentence time carefully. His plan was to leave the rigors of the city and travel upstate where he could camp in the open wilderness, free from confinement and the closeness of others. That light at the end of the tunnel was all he needed and the open space was to be his prime ingredient. He knew his tolerance of people, especially those who didn't value life, another's personal space, or the daily benefit of a cleansing shower, would be in short supply.

In prison he had avoided trouble. He kept to himself and, more importantly, he kept his mouth shut. These were traits that had aided him well before his incarceration.

Unfortunately while he was away, events transpired that changed his plans and affected his future. His mother was diagnosed halfway though his sentence with multiple sclerosis and required constant medical attention. T-bone's savings was soon depleted and by the time he stepped off the Greyhound bus three blocks from his mother's small wood framed house, the only thing he possessed in the world was his Bronco and the discharge check from the U. S. Bureau of Prisons for twelve hundred dollars, an amount that represented fewer than eleven cents per hour for his thirteen-year investment.

He looked down the dark alleys as he continued to cruise. That's where they hid, the night women of Bed Sty. They would stand close to each other, moving their extremities to keep warm. They wore small, revealing outfits as they exhaled warm breaths of steam. Most were black although that wasn't what he was after. Poor white trash was his flavor; the more tattoos and body piercings, the better.

As the traffic opened up, he took a tight right-hand turn and then he spotted her. She was a lone white girl in a crowd of blacks, wearing a pair of red shorts and a sequin tube top, all of which probably fit her well when she was twenty pounds lighter.

"Hey mista. What you lookin' fo' out here?" she asked, trying to sound as ghetto as possible.

"I think we both know what I'm looking for," T-bone replied.

"You need to be tha one who say it baby," she explained, standing back from the truck. "It be how I knows you ain't the police."

He liked her immediately. She was just what he'd been waiting for after thirteen years.

"A little fifty-fifty?" he asked.

"A hunded'," she replied confidently.

"A hundred?" T-bone bargained. "I got fifty bucks."

"Fifty fo' fifty baby. You want it all, it's gonna cost ya a benny."

"What's your name?"

"Marnie. What's yours?"

"My friends call me T-bone. How about seventy-five for all of it Marnie?"

"Works for me baby," she said climbing into the elevated front seat of the truck. "Where you planning on going with this thing mista?"

"Here and there," T-bone evaded.

"So…we gonna fuck o' what?" she asked. "Pull into that alley," the girl pointed to a dark space between two adjacent buildings as he complied. Once parked, T-bone reclined the seat as far back as it would go. The girl – Marnie – began to work as he closed his eyes. Her head bounced upon his lap as thirteen years of anticipation exploded and he let out a faint grunt.

"That was quick," she said with a swallow.

As he opened his eyes, a smile formed on his face. He had survived and now he would get back to work and rebuild that which he had lost.

"Sorry, it was great. And I just got out of the joint."

"Wow. I didn't know."

"Yeah, babe. I guess I won't be needing the other fifty," he said with an even bigger smile now.

"It's okay. I'll tell you what. You let me sit here a while wit' ya where it's warm and I'll give you a discount next time."

"I like the way you think Marnie."

"Really? You mean dat?"

"Yeah, I do."

"What you do time fo' anyways?"

"It's complicated."

"I hears that," she said, lighting a cigarette before seeing a man look in their direction from the end of the alley. "Oh shit!"

"Is that your…"

"Pimp? No. I ain't got no pimp. That be Young Jesus. He thinks he owns me but it ain't so."

"What's his problem?"

"He goes afta' the runaways, you know, from Jersey and shit. Hooks 'em up on crack and uses 'em 'til there ain't nothin left."

"Sick bastard," T-bone commented as the girl took a pen and wrote in the palm of his right hand.

"Here's my number if you...you know."

"Thanks Marnie."

"Hey, it ain't nothin' but a thang baby. Now write that down when you get home. Don't be jerkin' off wit' that hand and rub it off."

"I won't," T-bone laughed.

"Good... I'll be seein' ya," she said, and as fast as she had climbed into his truck, she jumped out and was walking back out of the alley and into the cold night leaving behind a smoky trail from her cigarette.

Chapter 5

4:00 AM
92 hours left

Sleep experts called it automatism but when fifty-four year old Melanie Greene awoke a few hours before dawn every morning at the same time, she called it her mental clock. She rolled over amidst the heavy covers and thousand thread count sheets confirming the time from a bright red LED digital clock on her nightstand. Then, almost instinctively, she grabbed her cell phone to see if there were any missed calls.

A storm front had moved in and ice had formed around the outside of her bedroom window. The top of her classic brownstone was in the path of some very cold air, making half of her room colder than the rest of the house. Still, she got up only wearing a pair of jogging shorts and a thin tee shirt. Her goal was to bump up the thermostat a couple of degrees. The home past her bedroom was warm and comfortable. As her daughter's career evolved so had the gifts of home improvement items over the last few years. The latest was wall-to-wall inlaid oak and cherry wood flooring that felt good against Melanie's bare feet.

As she squinted in the dark to adjust the wall-mounted dial, she felt something rub the back of her calf. Startled, she looked down.

"Trooper!" she whispered as loud as she could. "You scared the shit out of me."

Zoë's two-month-old Persian kitten looked up with a hungry meow. The pet was the product of an impromptu drive to the Pocano Mountains when, while driving, Zoë had seen the newborn kitten trying to cross three lanes of traffic. She had stopped, and with the assistance of a New York State Trooper who closed down the entire interstate, rescued the defenseless creature. In the end, Zoë got a new friend she named appropriately *Trooper* and the helpful public servant got an autograph.

"Didn't your mommy feed you?" Melanie asked as she walked towards her daughter's room. Trooper followed, obsessed with every step the woman's bare feet made on the wooden floor.

Of Zoë's faults, breaking her routine was not one of them. She was, as her mother described her, "predictable to a fault." Even her friends called her dependable and her director on the set found her to be prompt, reliable and ready to work. If Zoë was going to be later then 1:00 AM Melanie got a call. If she had a bad date, Melanie got a call. And if she was diverting, even the slightest bit from her daily routine, Melanie got a call. The two were, for lack of a better term, inseparable. This is why Melanie looked so shocked to see the door to Zoë's room open and her bed made and empty.

Zoë, since graduating from the Children's Professional High School in Manhattan, had only three serious boyfriends, serious on *her* personal scale which meant that they were in her life as long as it coincided with her future plans. Regardless, Melanie was always the first to know anything of importance, and when the precocious young woman would plan a breakup, she knew that too. Her daughter had grown accustomed to the control she possessed by safeguarding her emotions and fencing off her vulnerabilities, a lesson she learned from her first big love in college. He was a rugby player who was in the relationship for the sport of it. To Zoë, it was a valuable lesson learned. Her next was a front man for a local band that was just starting to hit it big. They broke it off after realizing that neither had the time to commit and did so as friends. Her last was a junior trader with an expansive Wall Street investment banking firm. At first she was flattered with his vast array of expensive gifts but became wary after he developed a possessive, controlling temper towards her. After several attempts to end the relationship, the young suit-clad man began following Zoë to her rehearsals, her home and to Evangeline's, where she was still working at the time. During their last conflict, the jealous lover burst into the restaurant during a Friday dinner rush where he found her seated with Roman at his table. Like an angry parent to a wandering child, he walked straight to Zoë and took her hand. She pulled back, frightened and shocked by his boldness. Roman intervened by grabbing his wrist. Nello followed with an even heavier hold on the young banker's shoulder. Later that night the man was treated for injuries sustained in what he described as a clumsy fall down a flight of stairs. Thirty-two black silk sutures, two broken ribs and a dislocated forefinger on his right hand later and he was never heard from again.

It was this incident that left an indelible watermark in her outlook of men and the relationships she had chosen to participate in. For the time being, Zoë Greene had decided that all men were a distraction, especially in a time when she craved simplicity like her baby kitten Trooper had once craved its mother's milk.

Chapter 6

6:10 AM
89 hours, 50 minutes left

Fitz hated hospitals. He had to endure a ritual though that made him visit New York Methodist twice a week. He tried to schedule the visits on Tuesday and Friday mornings primarily because his oncologist recommended that they needed to be spread as equally as possible. Fitz also liked the fact that he could go right back to work after the brutal infusions and the distraction took his mind away from the discomfort of the whole ordeal. His schedule at the precinct house was the standard Monday through Friday, 7:00 AM to 3:00 PM.

Fitz was a tough man by most standards. The chemotherapy beat him down though like nothing he had ever experienced. Still, twice a week he walked through the double doors and made his way to the sixth floor enduring the bitter smell of alcohol. This day was different though as he made a quick stop by the geriatric acute care ward.

"Hey Fitz," nurse Maria Gomez yelled out.

"How's she doing?"

"Tough night, but she'll live to see another day."

Fitz walked into the room where Emma Jean Stewart, the widow of his former partner, laid. At seventy she had seen a full life. She had been married to one man and from that union she bore twin sons.

"Two would be nice," Fitz said looking over at the aged woman that was sleeping quietly with the assistance of a constant supply of oxygen and a cocktail of IVs and other drugs.

"Two…?" the nurse asked.

"Two days Maria. It would be nice if she could see the year 2000."

"She won't know the difference hon."

"You've got my cell number if anything changes," Fitz reminded her.

"Right here," she said patting the open breast pocket of her oversized lime green scrub top.

"I had better get upstairs. They don't like to be kept waiting."

"Hey, let me know if you need me to come up and get a vein for you."

"You've got the touch Maria, that's for sure."

Ten minutes later Fitz was reminded why he'd grown to hate needles the way he did. In the past he hadn't minded the simple injections his chemotherapy required, but one of the side effects that developed was that his veins had become calloused and brittle. Getting the Teflon catheter to puncture the side of one of his vessels was like injecting a garden hose into an over-inflated party balloon and hoping it wouldn't burst. At best, the nurses on the eighth floor could get a patient's line with six painful tries. This day was not one of those *good* days though. Fitz smiled as Maria entered the ward.

"You needed to just ride up with me on the elevator," he said.

"What am I going to do with you?" she said with a smile, moving the other nurses aside. "I have really sick patients to tend to in my own corner of the world don't you know."

"Eight sticks and he wouldn't let us try anymore. He said to call you," a young blond tech from the IV team said.

"I want you to watch everything I do and practice with your next patient," Maria said, assuming her teacher mode.

"Yes ma'am."

"First, we need to loosen this damn tourniquet. Patients like these, no offense Fitz, can't handle that much blood pressure against the walls of the vein. You need to take it easy."

"That's my girl," Fitz said with a relaxed smile.

"But how will I find the vein?" the tech asked.

"It takes practice but in time you will be able to spot them at a glance," Maria said, holding Fitz's arm up to her. "Here, take your hand..."

The tech rubbed her soft palm across his forearm up towards his elbow.

"See? The pressure engorges the veins without putting too much pressure on the walls."

"Yeah but..."

"Mark the vein with a small pen and relax the pressure," Maria instructed, prepping the site with some alcohol before injecting the eighteen-gage needle, slipping the sharp tip below his dark skin. A small drop of blood formed at the insertion site as she slid the needle deeper into his flesh, gently probing for the vein. She watched closely for the blood flash that occurred inside the catheter's tip, a telltale sign that it was where it was supposed to be. Fitz just looked away and chewed on some ice chips to distract him from the sting.

"There we go," Maria said as the hollow plastic tip atop the catheter swelled with dark red blood.

"Thank you," Fitz said.

"I wish I could say it was my pleasure. You know I hate seeing you like this."

The tech secured the port in place with some hypoallergenic tape before connecting the plastic tubing that was attached to an IV bag. The fluid was filled with the alkylating agents that would hopefully change the cell structure of the tumor that was eating at his stomach. The problem was that these agents changed the delicate balance of electrolytes, many of which were responsible for the electrical functioning of the heart. As the heart strained, the patient would invariably feel the common side effects of the impending cardiogenic shock that included a non-rhythmic heartbeat, low blood pressure and extreme nausea in many cases. Of the patients that did not survive chemo, this was the stage that killed them.

"Hey, got any plans for the big new year?" Fitz asked with renewed enthusiasm.

"4:00 PM to midnight, house supervisor. I bet I don't get out of here until 2:00 AM," Maria answered with regret.

"Me too. I think every cop in the city is scheduled to be on duty."

"When aren't you on duty Fitz?" she asked sarcastically.

"The next day. I mean, I'm off on the first."

"Oh…"

"I was wondering…" Fitz said, feeling the poison feed his veins.

"Yes?"

"If you would like to…"

"Sure," she interrupted, "I'd love to."

"I didn't give you my plan."

You didn't have to. I've been waiting for you to ask me out for twenty-five years.

"Really?"

"Really."

"I guess I need to get better then…" Fitz admitted.

"You will," she affirmed. "So what big plans do we have for the first day of the millennium?"

"Well, after we junk all the computers in the house, I was thinking we could practice replacing our 19s with 20," he said before turning away from her.

"What is it?" she asked.

"Oh, nothing," he said looking away as he felt the surge of nausea infiltrate his core.

"Relax," she said, rubbing his back with comforting strokes. "Breathe easy Fitz, nice and slow."

He couldn't hold it back any longer as the contents of his stomach broached his throat and emptied into a waiting bedpan.

"Wow, that was colorful," she said.

Fitz chuckled as he cleaned his mouth and face.

"I'm sorry. I haven't done that in a while."

"So, tell me about this plan."

"A few of us from the precinct are going to cook some food, drink some beers, tell lies; you know, cop stuff."

"Sounds like a great way to welcome the new year."

"And watch the Rose Bowl of course," Fitz announced.

"Wouldn't miss it for the world," Maria agreed. She loved football.

"That's mandatory, as long as we're rooting for UCLA."

"Okay you trader. My mom is from Wisconsin, but I guess we can work on that."

"Hey Maria…"

"What is it Fitz?"

"Thanks," he said laying his head on the pillow, spent of all his available energy and that which lay in reserve. He closed his eyes and let the treatment take its course.

Chapter 7

6:52 AM
89 hours, 8 minutes left

Roman drove his new three-quarter ton Chevrolet pickup into the alley behind Evangeline's. He had made a stop by the 17th Street pier fish market and had filled half the bed with everything from hard shell mussels to squid for the restaurant's tantalizing calamari. His truck, like most manufactured that year, was equipped with automatic headlights. As he pulled down the dark alley they switched on, illuminating the shadows that were at the base of the tall buildings above. Suddenly a figure jumped from behind the dumpster. Expecting one of the many homeless men that fed on the restaurant's discards, he was caught off guard when a bright strobe exploded in front of his truck with a brilliant *SNAP*.

Roman jammed on the brakes with his foot and thrust open the door at the same time, catching the man with a fury of blunt force. The man, thin and about thirty, fell backwards into a mound of week-old gray snow that had lingered in the cold shadows.

"Don't!" the man pleaded.

"What the hell do you think you're doing?"

"I'm with *The Observer*. I've been waiting all night…"

"Waiting? For what?" Roman asked.

"Zoë. Zoë Greene," he answered as Roman shifted mental gears. "Don't kill me – oh my God!" the photog continued to plead as he shielded his face with his arms.

"Give me that damn thing," Roman ordered, grabbing the man's camera. "See this Fucko?" Roman announced as he slung the camera by its strap against the steel dumpster. It smashed into several pieces as the man ran out of the alley.

Inside, Roman stepped into the restaurant's freezer and inspected the unit's digital display that revealed the ambient air temperature, Freon levels, and power draw. With a quick glance he could see everything was running smoothly as the heavy door slammed shut behind him. Roman liked it in here. Ever since Vietnam he had never minded the cold and the constant hum of the compressor and air handlers seemed to drown out all of the outside noises. He also liked it because he could smoke his cigars at will in here and not risk bothering any of his customers.

After verifying his inventory with what was on the shelves, he grabbed the huge door latch and tried to exit. One of the inconsistencies of the large walk-in type freezers was that the locking mechanisms liked to stick. Roman hadn't had a problem with this one in months but a recent change in humidity combined with a lack of maintenance from the company that serviced the unit meant that he found himself briefly held captive. In his pragmatic nature, Roman simply stepped back, took a long drag from his cigar, and kicked the handle as the door flew open. In doing so, he thought back to the early days of the restaurant, back when it was called La Trottoria. An employee had locked himself in an older model of the same walk-in freezer for two days before being discovered. He was found cold, shivering and engorged with an abundant supply of hanging pork, chicken and beef.

Twenty minutes later Roman scanned the racks of provisions in the restaurant's non-refrigerated supply room. It was a continuation of his Tuesday morning ritual. Tall metal shelves stored everything from gallon cans of stewed tomatoes to heavy sacks of flour and Styrofoam takeout boxes. He studied each shelf, peering through a pair of wire-rimmed reading glasses with a cold Cojiba cigar perched in the corner of his mouth. Every item corresponded with a quantity listed on his printed Excel spreadsheet that was pinned to the aluminum clipboard he held in his left hand. In his right he handled the various items, checking the expiration dates and crosschecking the quantities with those that were listed on his supply report.

Since taking the restaurant over twenty-six years before, he made a steady effort to eliminate the large distributors by employing several of the smaller vendors, some only supplying one or two items. Even his produce came from three different purveyors, ensuring that they would always have a few different sources for the same essential items. This was crucial for a menu that was produce-heavy. Every week sixteen different reps stocked these shelves and made sure none of Roman's popular menu items would end up on the evening's "eighty-six" list. The practice also helped him keep a handle on his costs. It was an exercise in futility according to his father, who had Nello order twice what they needed. Back in the day, cases of raw provisions went out the front door as fast as they came in the back. It wasn't actually *stealing*, Ray Senior would justify. He considered it loyalty building that also helped the community. If there was a needy family in the district, Senior made sure they, at the very least, had the ingredients to put a meal on the table. After all, what did he care? The more supplies he ordered, the more he could justify in phony sales and the bolstered income on a set of books so doctored they smelled of alcohol. Not that the money that was washed through the restaurant made so much as a dent in the large surplus of cash that needed to be cleaned and accounted for. At the end of the day though, every little bit helped and the restaurant was no exception.

Roman looked over at 21. Sitting, hunched over a steaming cup of coffee was the heavy frame of Tommy "T-bone" Bonatrelli, a legend from Roman's younger days.

"I got him set up for you boss. I hope you don't mind," Nello said.

"No. Don't worry about it," Roman replied looking over at his guest who was spicing up his drink with the contents of a silver flask that the man had kept concealed within the confines of his jacket.

Tommy and Roman grew up together but when the latter enlisted, Tommy went to work for Ray Senior. T-bone was, for years, a loyal member of the family. Even his nickname came from his service to his fellow brothers who knew he could be counted on. One spring afternoon while making a pickup in the Borough of Queens, T-bone was ambushed by a small group of Genovesas, members of a rival family. With over three hundred thousand in a duffle bag, Tommy took a shot in the face and another in his left shoulder before plowing his 1976 Cadillac Deville into the side of his pursuer's car. The *T-bone* action pushed their Plymouth half a block before meeting the front end of a city garbage truck. All three men were killed instantly as the forks on the larger truck impaled the side of their sliding car. T-bone escaped before the cops arrived and delivered his money accounting for every dollar and, in doing so, became an instant street legend. To his close friends, T-bone's name was shortened even more to just *Bones*.

"Roman!" T-bone said, standing to hug his friend.

"Bones...you look good brotha!"

"Eat yet?" T-bone asked.

"No. It's early. You want some bruschetta with a little mozzarella?"

"You read my mind."

"Nello!" Roman said, raising a hand.

"Already on it boss," Nello replied as he headed towards the kitchen.

Roman lit two cigars and handed one to his friend across the table as he sat back into the soft leather upholstery. As the two relaxed, Roman looked over at T-bone who returned the glance and the two laughed.

"Mother of God. We missed you Bones."

"You don't know the half of it. Terre Haute was a hellhole. Now with all that terrorism shit the place is locked down tighter than Louisa Perez's pussy," T-bone expounded as the two chuckled.

"Wow…that tight, huh?" Roman replied, as they laughed some more. "So did the no-show work out at Hudson Produce?"

Roman had set up a job-on-paper for his friend with one of his purveyors. It was a condition of his parole and was the ideal arrangement. Hudson was to invoice the restaurant an extra amount for produce it didn't deliver. Evangeline's paid the bill and T-bone received a weekly paycheck complete with withholding taxes and inclusion in the company's health insurance plan. He was given the position of assistant territory manager over the southern half of Manhattan which, conveniently enough, included Roman's restaurant. This was critical since T-bone's parole included a condition that forbid him from associating with known criminal elements, except when the parolee was engaged in the course of gainful employment.

"Yeah, the job is great. Thanks," T-bone replied.

"Take a couple of days for yourself and then we'll find something for you to do."

"Whatever you need Roman, you know that."

"I know."

"Hey, how's your pop holdin' up?"

"He's doing okay…considering. It doesn't look good."

"I'm sorry man," T-bone answered as Roman got up.

"Hey, I've got to finish my order," Roman finished. "Relax, enjoy some food. We'll talk later."

"Thanks Roman."

* * *

As Roman finished his inventory he could hear the steady pounding of a woman's pumps through the bar and dining room. If T-bone was the calm, Melanie Greene was most certainly the storm. Over the years she had become hardnosed. As a woman of Polish and Jewish descent she was as shrewd as she was smart. Still, Melanie was taller and possessed an attractive smile although she seldom used it. Her hips, like many women her age, had begun to spread despite her daily exercise routine and restrictive diet. She had been married once but after her husband's death, she never took another. There was only Zoë and for her daughter she devoted her time and talents.

While her daughter's talent was the prime ingredient for her success, it was Melanie's management that introduced her to the world. It was Melanie who arranged for her daughter to be represented by one of the most powerful agents in Los Angeles. Agents were, after all, strange creatures. As Zoë had proclaimed at an awards show, "this is for my agent who believed in me when everyone else did." Melanie, her manager, believed in her when no one knew her name or even wanted to. She had beaten the streets with Zoë in tow, to auditions and casting calls in hopes of landing the prime role that would get her cataloged in the rolodexes of the better casting agents around town.

"Hello Roman. We've got a problem," Melanie said, walking into the empty dining room and towards the restaurant's small office.

Chapter 8

8:27 AM
87 hours, 33 minutes left

In a rented apartment high atop Greenwich Street, two Diplomatic Security Service agents stood watch. Forty-three year old Special Agent Joel Kenyon brewed a pot of fresh coffee while his partner, a DSS intern, calibrated the cameras that were erected and aimed out the flat's large bay window at one target, the restaurant Evangeline's.

"I've been here a week and, pardon me for saying, but I don't see the point," the intern said as he signed off on the video checklist and logged his ID into an adjacent computer.

"It's complicated. Just remember that what you see here, stays here," Agent Kenyon explained.

"How is this place an annex to anything? It looks like another guinea joint to me," he said as Kenyon looked over with a disappointing glance. "What? I'm a guinea on my mother's side," the intern said with a smile.

"Look, most of this is above your clearance level so I'll be vague. That restaurant down there has been the headquarters for an organized worldwide syndicate that traces back to the old country," Kenyon explained.

"Mafia?" the intern asked with raised eyebrows.

"Call it what you want. Mafia, la cosa nostra, the mob...some of the biggest names in OC walk through those doors."

"I get it, and because they are classified as an annex of the Italian Consulate, the FBI can't conduct surveillance or tap the phones... it's hands off," the intern concluded.

"You didn't hear that from me," Kenyon said with a stern look.

"And you're not regular DSS, are you? No one I've talked to has ever heard of you before," the intern speculated.

"You *definitely* didn't hear *that* from me!" Kenyon replied.

"DSS can tap the phone, spy into the windows, enter at will and do it all in the name of diplomatic safety. It's beautiful."

"It's not that easy. We have to be careful. I think I read someplace that you worked at the Pentagon when you were discharged from the Marines?"

"Yeah, why?"

"You have a top secret clearance, that's why you're here."

"So are you DSS or FBI?"

"Last week I worked for the FBI, this week I'm DSS. Can't be both son."

"I get it. But what can you do with the evidence. It can't be admissible."

"Evidence? It's not about evidence; it's about intelligence. And staying one step ahead and three steps behind...of the mob that is."

"What's left of the mob you mean..."

"That's right, but for every member we put away another one gets out. It's up to us to monitor their movements. If a paroled member enters that establishment, well let's just say we can perceive that as a threat to diplomatic security and notify his P.O."

"Get 'em violated...good plan," the intern said.

"We'll see. Haven't tried it yet."

"So we're the guinea pigs?"

"Interesting choice of words," Kenyon remarked.

Joel poured two cups of steaming coffee. While the apartment had electricity, it didn't have any heat. Other agents had brought small space heaters but they were prone to blow the circuit breakers because of all the other sophisticated electronic equipment. The fuse panel was four floors down in the building's basement. All the up and down was starting to draw attention so the call was made to, as the memo read, *restrict the use of supplemental heating equipment.*

"Hey, who's this guy?" the intern asked as Kenyon joined him at the window.

"Bingo!" the senior agent said with enthusiasm. "Speak of the devil…our first subject."

"What? Who?"

"Thomas Bonatrelli, the guy they call T-bone. Released last week from the Terre Haute Federal Detention Center."

"What now…? Call his P.O.? Arrest him?"

"Nope. Let's sit tight for a few days and see what develops."

Chapter 9

8:41 AM
87 hours, 19 minutes left

One of the side effects of Fitz's chemotherapy was that it made him overheat in a way that his face became flushed and sweat began to bead on his brow. While many preferred to be pampered with ice chips and wet hospital towels, the seasoned detective's cure was to get dressed and walk the cold streets of Brooklyn.

This was where it all started for him as a uniformed patrol officer from the 78th Precinct. As he stepped through the automatic sliding glass doors at New York Methodist and onto the wet sidewalk, he felt the cold air enter his lungs. The air and sun were as rejuvenating as the vitamin-enriched smoothies the staff had him drink after his infusion. Fitz had never considered himself to be claustrophobic, but lately he felt his anxiety levels rise every time he walked through those hospital doors. It was a phenomenon he didn't understand. He had been a familiar fixture at Methodist, going back thirty years to when the six-hundred-bed facility was known as the Methodist Hospital of Brooklyn. It was his lifelong friend Maria Gomez who made all of his latest visits bearable and now she, after decades of dithering, was going to meet him for a social gathering. It was almost as if being given months to live finally made him appreciate all those that had always been within his reach.

With renewed vigor Fitz headed north on 7th Street. The terrain had changed considerably since he walked these streets as a beat cop. Despite the changes, there was one block that seemed to stay the same, withstanding the rigors of time. He didn't know what drew him back there, especially today. He hadn't been in that alley since that day, the day that changed his life forever and ended the life of his partner. Now Captain Stanley Fitzgerald found himself staring down that dark musty corridor, an evil place that lived in the far reaches of his memory.

Fitz stood motionless for a few minutes. Ice and snow hung from the fire escapes, just like they did that fateful day twenty-five years ago. He took a step and then two. *It was all the same*, he thought to himself. Despite the massive changes to this part of Brooklyn with the redevelopment projects and community architectural initiatives, this small patch of concrete, brick and mortar seemed just like it did back then. He could picture the red Valentine's decorations in the garbage cans sprinkled with white snow, the dripping ice from the overhangs above, and the body of the nursing student Bettina Cooper lying on the ground, seizing from a single gunshot wound to the back of her head.

The detective captain continued deeper into the alley, walking slowly as his heart started to beat faster. He could feel the carotid pulse in his neck beat against the knit collar of his turtleneck shirt. Still, he walked further, looking behind each dumpster and in to the many recessed doorways, like a child playing hide and seek. A subconscious reflex took over and he felt his right hand go down and rest on the rubber grip handle of his Glock 21 automatic pistol that was strapped to his waist under his jacket. His pulse was racing now. He was getting closer. It was almost as if a replay had been extricated from the deepest portions of his memory. He heard and felt the shot ring out. “Bill,” he called out in a whisper. Then without warning a consuming wave of nausea took over and Fitz bent down, expelling the contents of his irritated stomach for the second time of the day, over the snow-covered ground. He dropped down to his knees, shivering with a stabbing, painful cold that rocked his bones and joints. He grabbed his chest with one hand and whipped the vomit from his mouth with the other. Fitz hadn’t vomited in twenty-five years and never had he done it twice in one day. The first was a swift result of his chemo. The second was – *what?* He questioned himself. *A panic attack?* He sat there for what seemed like hours. In time the feeling passed but the memory and the desire to do something about it had been reignited.

Chapter 10

8: 55 AM
87 hours, 5 minutes left

"Roman, we've got a problem," Melanie Greene announced.

"What now?" he grumbled.

"Have you seen this?" Melanie asked, tossing the morning's copy of *The Observer* onto the cluttered office desk. *The Observer* was a New York based celebrity gossip paper that had a daily release and a national circulation of over twenty million copies. While most didn't take the stories seriously, the attention the outlet generated was primarily negative. The articles the paper published had been designed to do one thing – sell more papers. Whether it was at a grocery store checkout line or a street side newsstand, the pictures and provocative headlines did just that. They caught people's attention, people who, by reading the libelous half-truths and innuendos went on with their days, feeling better about themselves in a world where the reality of a few was determined by the perception of many.

Most of the celebrities that had been profiled in the paper were happy to be there. Negative attention was, after all, still attention. West Coast publicists, as a rule, adored the tabloids. "The time to worry is when they *stop* writing about you," most would tell their clients. For Zoë Green, negative attention was just that, *negative,* and she didn't want anything to do with *The Observer* or any other paper that boosted its circulation by invading the lives of others, especially her own. For Roman, papers like these had no place in his life and could only cause serious trouble for him and his family, especially now.

He picked up the poorly printed paper and came face-to-face with the front page that bore his and Zoë's pictures, which had been positioned next to each other under the striking headline and corresponding caption.

Strange Bedfellows

> Zoë Greene, star of the hit-rated NBC crime drama, *The Prosecutor*, along with reputed underworld boss, Roman Sabarese, appear to be quite the couple. The two have been inseparable and sources close to the Greene camp say they are involved and their relationship is growing. Greene's publicist was contacted for this piece and had no comment but *The Observer* did learn that the twenty-four year old actress's financial dealings could fall under the scrutiny of the Federal Bureau of Investigation who routinely tracks associates of organized crime figures like Sabarese, both reputed and confirmed.

"Max will be here in an hour. I'll get an injunction filed against these hacks," Roman said.

"An injunction? Roman, the paper is already on the street. Do you know what this could do to her?"

"No one could actually believe this nonsense," Roman suggested.

"Really? And what planet are you living on? The President of the United States can bang a girl half his age. Why can't the public assume you, the Prince Don of New York, would be morally above his actions?"

"It's rubbish," Roman insisted.

"You and I know that."

"And Max and Nello," Roman added.

"Great Roman. Good to know that Zoë's reputation is safe with the four of us. Hell, that just leaves the other four million in the city to contend with. No problem," she answered sarcastically as she rested her tired face in the palms of her hands.

"Those damn paparazzi," Roman mumbled.

"What?"

"I had a run-in with a photographer this morning. He was staking out the back alley," Roman admitted.

"Great!"

"I don't think he'll be back," Roman said.

"You didn't…?" Melanie asked in a concerned, softer voice.

"No! But he got the message," Roman said with a confident smile.

"Well tough guy, to make matters worse, Zoë didn't come home last night."

"I saw her up to eleven or so."

"What time do you think they drop those papers on the streets?" Melanie asked.

"I don't know. Two or three?"

"You don't think she saw a copy? Where was she headed?"

"I don't know. I got busy with a broken exhaust fan. By the time we got the damn thing fixed she was gone. Maybe she hit some of the clubs and stayed at a friend's place."

"Shit! She probably walked out into the street just in time to see this crap," Melanie stressed, grabbing the rumpled paper. "I'm concerned."

"She's a kid Mel. And she's living the dream," Roman assured her.

"You don't understand. That child doesn't do anything without letting me know first. Something's wrong. I just know it. Did you know she's got a stalker?"

"What? When?"

"This guy, Andrew Schultze. He's a real piece of work. A skinhead, white supremacist type. I guess he disapproves of Zoë's racial status."

"Too bad for him."

"It's not that easy. He's called the house a few times. And then…" she explained as she reached into the pocket of her long overcoat and pulled out a small rope noose. "This was left on the front stoop of our home. Our *home* Roman! This freak knows where we live!"

"What do you know about this guy?"

"He lives in Queens. Here's his address and phone number," she replied, handing over a small piece of paper.

"Let me do some checking. Keep your phone close."

"Always," she replied, patting the side of her purse.

Chapter 11

9:18 AM
86 hours, 42 minutes left

Roman Sabarese was by reputation, a made guy. Now that his father was in prison, he was the head of his family's made guys. His position was by default, like the prince that becomes the king of a country. He didn't work for it or deserve it nor even wanted to deserve it, although his family was not the empire it once was. In the seventies and eighties his father's reach had extended to the west coast and beyond but it was now limited to the five boroughs of the city. And now, with his father in Danbury, it was all he could do to maintain the family's slipping grip on an ever-changing economy in a city that grew more technological every year. "The days of cracking a man's skull open with a crowbar in broad daylight are over," Nello Falcone used to say.

The City of New York *alone* employed over three thousand closed circuit television cameras and a small army to watch them. With the advent of the Internet, thousands more *unofficial* cameras peered into every alley, backstreet and intersection, giving those who watched them an unobstructed view of the shadows and those who used to lurk in them. As *Time* magazine had written, "technology killed the mob."

With this advent, the federal government's power grew exponentially. Wiretaps were initiated with the click of a mouse and judges became available around the clock for impromptu search warrants that could be emailed directly to the scene of a criminal probe. Despite all of this, the real threat came in the form of DNA technology and its increasing acceptability as evidence in the federal court process. Something as small as a human hair could now be used to tie a wise guy to a crime scene and could link him to everything from a simple assault to a compound murder.

Roman sat at his table as he dialed Zoë's cell phone.

"It's me...can't talk right now. Please leave a message and I'll get back to you as soon as I can. Ciao."

Frustrated, he hit the *end* button and tossed the phone down on the tablecloth. *When did she start saying ciao?* he thought to himself. *Who was this girl becoming?*

"Hey Nello, come here for a second," Roman said, motioning his manager over. "I'm gonna need your help with something. Call Bones back in."

"What's up boss?"

"Melanie Greene just told me that Zoë's missing. No word since yesterday."

"I just saw her last night."

"Yeah, until eleven or so which means two things: she left when we got tied up with that damn exhaust fan and *we* were the last people to see her."

"What do you think?"

"It's probably nothing. It might even be related to this crap," Roman suggested, tapping his finger on the morning's edition of *The Observer* that Melanie had brought him. "But we had better play it safe."

"Tell me what to do," Nello offered.

"Go here and talk to this guy Andrew Schultze. Word is he's had an unusual attraction to our Zoë," he said, handing Nello the piece of paper Melanie had prepared.

"Got it. I'll call Bones right now," Nello replied.

"Also, I've been thinking about this Greenwich attacker thing."

"The Greenwich rapist that's been in the papers?" Nello answered as he put both hands on the side of Roman's table.

The Greenwich rapist had been a threatening menace that was terrorizing the women of the Tribeca district for over three years. Four young women, all of whom were avid fitness buffs, had gone missing and were later found dead, violated, and their bodies mutilated. They had been found in back alleys with their throats slashed and still wearing their fitness outfits.

"So, do you think this guy has anything to do with Zoë?" Roman asked.

"I don't even want to think about it. If anyone hurt that precious girl, I'll..."

"Focus Nello, come on!"

"Sorry boss."

"Can we find this other guy?"

"Let me do some checking. I'll see who the cops are watching."

"Let's get him before they do," Roman insisted. "Hey, by the way. Where the hell is Max? He was supposed to be here twenty minutes ago."

"You want me to call him?" Nello asked.

"No, I'll do it."

Max Weintraub was the only member of the family that wasn't Italian. He was, however, a trusted consigliore of sorts, an accountant and an attorney with a law degree from Harvard. It was his job to crunch the numbers and make sure the different Sabarese ventures made money, on and off the spreadsheets. He was originally hired in the late seventies by Ray Senior and had been rewarded well over the years. His investments were solid and his advice was golden. Had it not been for Max's addiction to gambling and his recent divorce, he would have been a rich man.

At sixty-two, he was living in a Staten Island rented flat paying six thousand dollars a month in court ordered alimony and in debt to Roman for another one hundred and forty thousand. For accomplishing so much for so many, it was a bitter disappointment to himself that his personal financial life was bleeding so much red ink.

As he approached table 21 Max tried to, as he always had, fit his rotund belly into the half round booth, carrying a cup of scalding coffee, a brief case, and a stack of files under his arm.

"Sorry I'm late," Max apologized.

"Where are we with Dubai?" Roman asked.

"Looking good boss. I got an email from the site manager and they are finished with sixty of the eighty-four crane pads for phase one."

The Dubai project had been Roman's brainchild. Having seen the future of international commerce and the gross amounts of freight it created, he took a bet investing a large portion of the Sabarese bank in a shipping port to be located in Dubai, a small Middle Eastern state located in the United Arab Emirates. In the initial phase, eighty-four permanent gantry cranes were to be constructed along six deep-water canals. Upon completion, each gantry would be capable of loading or unloading two hundred fifty-three-foot containers each shift, three shifts a day, operating around the clock, seven days a week. Unlike many of the American projects the family had been a part of, the newly formed Dubai syndicate was ahead of schedule and six percent under budget.

"The Chinese still on time to deliver the first set of gantries?" Roman asked.

"They are sitting in pieces on the dock in Tianjin," Max replied. "As soon as we get the word from the erector, our shipper will arrange the boats. They should be operational three weeks after they arrive in the UAE."

"Great. Finally, some good news," Roman said, grabbing a notebook. "Let's change gears for a second."

"Hey, about the money I owe…"

"No Max, it's not that. Senior and I have decided to make some major changes to the, shall I say, *structure* of our business. It's been in the works and now I think the time has come to implement what I believe will be a new course for us all," Roman explained, again tapping his finger on the newspaper that was in front of him, pointing out the picture of himself that graced the front page of *The Observer.*

"Okay?" Max questioned, wondering where his boss was going with this.

"I…*we* decided that it would be better for everyone involved if we allowed our captains to stand out," Roman announced, waiting for his advisor's response.

"Wow," Max replied, as this was the least of his list of expectations. "It's good, on one hand. Timing couldn't be better. It's a gamble on the other. You will lose control over what has been a lucrative position."

"You know I don't care about that."

"I know Roman, but you have to remember - this thing of ours is a lot bigger than just you. What were Senior's thoughts?"

"You know my father. Anything to set the stage for a release," Roman replied, shaking his head. "At the end of the day we need to protect what we already have. The best defense for people like us is to stop doing what people like us do."

"Easier said than done."

"What do we do anymore Max? Really…we're just the collectors."

"You gotta admit…it's not a bad place to be in life," Max reasoned with a chuckle.

"Everything has its price," Roman justified.

"So where do we go from here?"

"The plan is to collect six months worth of earnings in advance from all the captains. Deadline will be the end of the year."

"This year? Shit boss. That's not a lot of time."

"Fuck 'em. They pay or it goes up to the next guy in line. I want this done so I can start focusing on our future business."

"What about the Russians?"

"Not my problem. I can't tell you how unnerving it is to be the lightning rod for this entire family. I'm done here."

"A well-paid lightning rod I might add," Max smiled.

"Long range Max. Technology is killing this thing of ours. It's not like it used to be. Hell, you can't take a piss anymore without getting caught on half a dozen cameras."

"I'll put some numbers together and send them over by this evening."

"Sorry. I need them in an hour. This is going to happen rather quickly. Thanks Max…and good work with Dubai," Roman finished, taking another sip of coffee.

Chapter 12

10:32 AM
85 hours, 28 minutes left

Special Agent Joel Kenyon and his DSS intern fought the urge to go back to sleep after an early morning of inactivity and subsequent boredom. At 10:32 AM, Evangeline's, the restaurant that doubled as an annex to the Italian Consulate, was closed and wouldn't open its doors for business for another thirty minutes.

As the Resident Agent in Charge, Kenyon had been appointed lead agent by his field SAC to oversee the foundation that would become the final case against the Sabarese family. This post was not without its own balancing act. As an FBI agent, his actions were limited by the diplomatic status that Evangeline's possessed. As a DSS agent, his new temporary post, he could dig deeper and survey the faux annex under the auspices of Diplomatic Security and Safety. To him, it didn't matter. Ray Sabarese Senior and anyone connected to him was a part of a wide-reaching criminal enterprise and it was his job, whether it be as an FBI agent or as a DSS au pair, to employ any and all resources necessary to complete the task at hand, resources that could be used to end the Sabareses with the eventual goal of reducing organized crime in New York City, the tri-state area, and across the country.

He felt himself nod off one more time and then it happened. Like an angler whose fishing rod began to bend, Kenyon's head popped up.

"What do we have here?" he said aloud, startling his younger partner.

"I'm sorry…I must have dozed off," the intern replied, blinking his eyes in an attempt to wake himself completely.

Kenyon grabbed a pair of field glasses and watched closely as the restaurant manager Nello Falcone unlocked the front door from inside to accept three visitors donning great coats.

"Jackpot!" Kenyon blurted out as the intern watched through the tripod-mounted viewfinder of an SLR camera. "Start shooting. Get as much as you can."

"Who are they?" the intern asked as he clicked the shutter repeatedly.

"Upper level management for the Sabarese family. You are about to witness a sit-down my young friend."

"Jesus."

"Just keep shooting," Kenyon instructed as he picked up his cell phone with a free hand and speed dialed the first number on his list. "This is RAC Joel Kenyon, I need to speak to te SAC Pat Stephens please."

"Back alley is clear," the intern reported.

"Pat, it's Joel, we've got a sit-down," Kenyon said into the phone.

Special Agent In Charge Pat Stephens was a former federal prosecutor who had broken ranks to join the FBI and was eventually enlisted as the head of the city's organized crime unit. His men had been spearheading the Sabarese investigation.

"Who are the players?" Stephens asked.

"Looks like John Ciasuli, Paulo Alcone and a third guy I've never seen before."

"Is Roman in the restaurant?"

"I saw him enter from the rear at 6:30 AM, just like he does every morning."

"This could be what we've been waiting for."

"What I would give for some audio," Kenyon lamented.

"And you know better. You want to violate the European Diplomatic Pact?"

"It was more of a wish Pat."

"I usually keep those to myself. Who else is there?"

"Besides Falcone, just Tommy Bonatrelli, Devon the dishwasher, and some of the kitchen staff."

Chapter 13

10:33 AM
85 hours, 27 minutes left

Meetings of this caliber were rare but occasionally necessary. As the entourage passed through the bar, Nello and Bones stood back and watched. Leading the pack was John Ciasuli, a well-dressed man of three hundred and fifty pounds. "Big John," as friends knew him, had a reputation that was bigger than life on the streets of Brooklyn. He had been a loyal captain to Roman's father since the late sixties and was a solid earner, managing the family's vast statewide bookmaking operation. Big John exchanged nods with the bartender as he passed. He was a personable man, a caring member of the community and a regular fixture at Saint Augustine Church on Brooklyn's 6th Avenue.

Behind him was Sullivan Scoliari, a guy most would call "the typical Italian." He had a stocky build and jet-black hair that was combed back with an excess of greasy gel. "Sully," as he was called on the street, was Big John's enforcer; a one-man collection agency that went after the deadbeats that liked to bet, but hated to cover.

Bringing up the rear was Paulo "Pauly" Alcone, a short, round man whose head was just five feet six inches from the ground. Pauly was in charge of all union construction contracts in the states of New York, New Jersey, and Connecticut.

The three men sat in the round booth with Pauly on one side and Sully and Big John on the other. Roman sat in the middle, a position he had been getting used to as of late.

"Would anyone like a drink?" Devon the dishwasher asked.

"A double scotch for me," Pauly requested.

"All around Devon," Roman added.

"'Cept for you Mr. Roman."

"Just some more coffee," Roman said, turning to Pauly. "So what's the big problem that can't wait until next year?"

"This fucking guy roughed up the wrong man!" Pauly launched, pointing at Sully.

"Oh, you got some nerve…" Sully yelled back.

"Gentlemen. I will not have you arguing like school kids. Jesus! Show some restraint," Roman interjected.

"Roman, it's an honest mistake," Big John reasoned. "Sully was just doin' his job goin' afta' dis guy Richard somethin'"

"Richard Valella - you know the guy Roman. He's been skating for nine months now. The asshole owes us seventy large," Sully answered.

"So our friend Sully here goes to Passaic Building Supply and starts to rough this guy up. The owner of the business, Anthony Roldino, tries to break it up and gets his teeth knocked out," Big John explains.

"And a broken colla' bone. Don't forget that Johnny!" Pauly insisted. "Collas hurt like shit an' you can't do nothin' 'bout 'em."

"So help me out…who is this Roldino guy?" Roman asked.

"Anthony Roldino is married to Gina Scoliari Roldino. He's Pauly's brother-in-law. Now his sista' is bitchin' at him day and night."

"She won't let me sleep Roman, Jesus!" Pauly pleaded.

"Did you offer to buy him some new teeth?" Roman asked.

"One hundred percent and then some," Sully replied. "What else can I do?"

"One hundred percent my ass! What about the therapy?"

"Therapy?" Sully yelled. "I don't call a week in da Pocanos no fuckin' therapy."

"Pauly," Roman said with a sideways look.

"You get your teeth knocked out and try to recuperate at home," Pauly said with a smirk.

"Pauly," Roman said a little louder.

"Okay. Fuck the therapy," he conceded.

"Pauly, really, I'm sorry. I didn't know," Sully repeated.

"Yeah, yeah, yeah. Just be more careful next time, capisce?"

"Pauly, get your brother-in-law fixed up and bring him and your sister over here for dinner one night next week. It's on me," Roman suggested.

"Better stock up on some straws," Big John said with a smile.

"Oh, we can joke about it now motha fucker," Pauly said, shaking his head with a smile as he pointed towards Sully. "What the hell was little Anthony thinking? Gina beats the shit outta him all the time. Look at this guy Sully, he's built like a freight train."

"Let's put this thing to bed, okay?" Roman suggested.

"Sorry Roman, Pauly," Sully said, reaching over to shake his adversary's hand.

"Now that's the spirit," Big John said.

As the three guests relaxed and sipped their scotch, Roman cleared his throat as everyone looked in his direction.

"Look, there is something else I wanted to talk to you guys about," he said, commanding everyone's undivided attention. "I talked to Senior and we both agreed that it's time for you guys to stand out."

"What?" Pauly said in shock. "Shit Roman."

"If that's what the old man wants," Big John added as though he was expecting it.

"It is, and I want this settled before you guys leave here. I want us all to enter the new millennium with a fresh outlook and a new direction."

"What you got in mind Roman, if I may ask?" Pauly questioned.

"Max threw some numbers together based on what your juice has been over a six month period. That's it. Pay us the six months by the end of the year and you're out. John, you're at one point seven and Pauly, you owe nine hundred large."

"I don't know Roman," Pauly hemmed.

"Pauly, this is a gift," Roman added.

"It is," Big John said. "Count me in."

"I guess I can make it work," Pauly conceded.

"Hey Pauly, I can always buy your share and you can work for me," Big John added with a smile.

"No thanks wise guy. I'll get you the money by Friday Roman," Pauly answered.

"Thanks guys. You made this very easy and it won't go unnoticed."

"How's the old man holdin' up?" Sully asked.

"He's hanging in there Sully, thanks for asking."

"Hey, here's to Ray Senior," Big John said, holding up his glass of scotch.

"To Senior!" Pauly and Sully repeated as all three downed their glasses and Roman watched with a flat smile.

"One more thing boys. I've got a small personal problem I need some help with," Roman said.

"Hey Roman, does it got to do with that maggot paper *The Observer*?" Sully asked.

"Yeah, I saw that shit. The nerve…" Big John added.

"Yes and no. Zoë didn't come home last night and her mom is pretty worried. She's been out of pocket for twelve hours now. It's not like her."

"Shit Roman. You don't think anything's happened, do you?" Pauly asked.

"We don't know. Do me a favor and check around. See what you can find out okay? Call me or Nello with anything."

"I'll make some calls Roman," Big John said.

"Me too," Pauly added.

"We need to check all the pervs in the area. They got lists for that shit you know. On the Internet and all," Sully said.

"Thanks guys," Roman finished with sincerity.

Chapter 14

10:54 PM
73 hours, 6 minutes left

Bones' 1986 Ford Bronco bounced over the fused concrete panels with sharp repetitive thuds that occurred at a rate of two every second. It was a sensation that most in the tri-state area were used to. The Jersey Turnpike portion of Interstate Ninety-Five was elevated in sections and these bridges were known to settle and do so without any regard for balance or symmetry; the soft, wet ground the freeway was built over made this worse. It was road surfaces like this that made heavier cars more popular, cars like Cadillacs, Lincolns and Buicks acted more like boats and floated over the uneven terrain with suspensions that absorbed the micro-bumps like a knife slicing through warm butter. The Bronco however, possessed none of these qualities and Nello, who was strapped into the passenger seat, couldn't wait for their jaunt to the Meadowlands to be over.

Restrained in the cargo section and wrapped in a concealing blanket was twenty-eight year old Andrew Schultze. As bad as the ride was for Bones and Nello in the front of the tight Bronco, it was three times as bad for their prisoner in the back. Like the ride in the extreme rear of a school bus, the rear of Bones' Bronco surged vertically with every concrete joint, to the point of making the confined skinhead sick to his stomach.

Nello knew they were getting close to their destination when the top of Giants Stadium came into view. Like an oasis, the stadium was not only home to the famous Giants football team, but it was also the host for scores of concerts like Bruce Springsteen and George Thorogood, both of whom were Jersey natives. Besides the arena and an adjacent entertainment park, the Meadowlands was just that, a huge wet meadow of saw grass and water, New Jersey's version of the Everglades.

As the Bronco glided down the off ramp, Bones made an abrupt U-turn and parked under the elevated highway. Seconds later, Nello dropped the back tailgate and lifted the blanket to expose Schultze's bald head and bold, wide open blue eyes.

"Enjoy the ride Andrew? I know I did," Nello said sarcastically, looking over at Bones. Schultze grunted, his mouth bound with gray duct tape.

"Let me help you with that," Bones said, ripping the bands from around his face.

"What the fuck?" Schultze yelled.

"Hey, watch the language. Do you blow your boyfriend with that mouth?" Nello asked with a crooked smile.

"When I get out of this, you guys…"

"Chill the fuck out Adolph," Bones replied. "Tell us what we want to know and my partner and I might let you keep your cock and balls. Got it?"

"Shit! Mother…kyke…Jew fucker!" Schultze yelled like a crack addict with Tourette's syndrome, panting to the point of exhaustion. His face had turned red and the backpressure of his violent yelling had forced copious amounts of mucus to flow from his mouth and nose.

"You know what they say Andrew…anger is a carcinogen. I'd hate to see you contract, you know, something testicular."

"Not to worry partner. At this rate he's not gonna have any balls to get…to get… hey, what happens when you get testicular cancer?"

"You don't catch it. It's not contagious," Nello added.

"You develop a tumor you idiot," Schultze said.

"Now that wasn't very nice. He was just looking out for your balls," Nello said.

"Yeah Adolph," Bones added as he pulled out a razor sharp fillet knife and sliced through the top of Schultze's head, down to his hard skull. Blood started to flow down both sides of his freshly shaved head.

"Next one takes out an eye," Nello said as Schultze sat silent, calculating the level to which his predicament had just escalated. "We don't have much time Andy. The scalp is very vascular and, judging from your level of agitation, I'd say you'll bleed to death in about five minutes. Tell us what we want and we'll deliver you to the best hospital in the city."

"You guinea fuckers think you're so…" Schulze spouted as Bones sliced another deep furrow into his scalp.

"Shit! Okay! What do you want?"

"What do you know about Zoë Green?" Nello asked.

"What? Is that what this is all about? Shit! I was just pissed off. I see she's banging one of your wop buddies. I was just running my mouth man."

"We heard you took her some place."

"That's a lie! No way. I never even met her. I mean, yeah, I saw her on the street and shit, but that's it."

"Why did you call her house and say the things you did?" Nello asked.

"And why did you leave a toy noose on her doorstep?" Bones added.

"Because she's a cunt! All righteous! Thinks she's better than everyone else. Shit, she's the Jew! She's the nigger! Double whammy baby!"

"I don't like your answers Adolph," Bones said as he plunged the knife straight into the young man's left eye. As he pulled it out, a mixture of blood and clear optic fluid flowed down Schultze's face.

"Oh my god! That was my eye! Oh my god! Now I'm really gonna get mad!"

"This guy's gonna die from terminal stupidity," Nello said, looking over at his partner. "Finish him."

Bones yanked Schultze the rest of the way out of the back of his Bronco, letting him fall the three feet to the hard packed dirt below.

"Oh God, no, don't..." Schultze yelled for the last time as Bones delivered one last plunge of the knife to the back base of the skinhead's skull. The young man started to seize violently and then, as though he was a wind-up toy that had run out of energy, he stopped, still, quiet and complete.

Chapter 15

Wednesday, 12:38 AM
71 hours, 22 minutes left

As the elevator door closed behind him, Roman unlocked the one dead bolt to the front door of his Park Avenue apartment. His Korean housekeeper had gone through the place earlier in the day and it smelled of the fresh lilac furniture polish she had used.

Roman kicked off his black orthopedic shoes and walked through to his kitchen, grabbing a cold bottle of Evian mineral water from the refrigerator. This was his favorite part of the day, though it was hard for him to relax with Zoë still unaccounted for. With a quick click of the remote, the TV in his living room came to life rebroadcasting an earlier show on CNN and the familiar raspy voice of Larry King.

"Mister Greenspan, what does the financial community have to say about the Y2K threat?" the seasoned interviewer asked his guest.

"I used to write those programs back in the sixties and seventies and was proud of the fact that I was able to squeeze a few elements of space out of my program by not having to put a nineteen before the year…" Alan Greenspan answered.

"So, when did we drop the ball?"

"It's not like we didn't know this day would come."

"Yeah, but why couldn't the problems have been addressed when the programs were originally written?"

"It's all about space Larry. Our goal at the time, like I just said, was to code as much data in as little space as possible. I think most of us just assumed that the hardware, as a whole, would have more capacity and then the changes could be made at that time. The problem is that the time is now and the powers that be have been procrastinating."

"Internationally, the price tag is estimated at three hundred billion dollars. That's a third of a trillion. We're not talking about pocket change here," King added.

"As computer hardware evolved so did the demands of this newer space-consuming software. The Y2K issue was always passed to the backburner in favor of bigger pictures and streaming video. That was our nation's priority, from the developer right down to the end user. We are all complicit here," Greenspan rationalized.

With the press of a button the screen went blank again as Roman grabbed for his cell phone. He dialed Zoë's number for the thirtieth time in forty-eight hours.

"It's me...can't talk right now. Please leave a message and I'll get back to you as soon as I can. Ciao," the announcement message repeated as Roman tossed the phone onto his couch. As soon as it bounced off the upholstery it began to ring.

"Zoë?" Roman asked.

"No boss, it's me," Nello announced. "It was a dead end."

"What about the warning?"

"No need. It's a done deal," Nello advised.

"Really?"

"Really. Our friend took care of that. It's all for the better."

"What do we do now?"

"I'm going to check on this other thing. I'll let you know how things turn out when it's done," Nello said as Roman ended the call.

With all the talk on the Larry King show about computers and the potential consequences, Roman thought he would search what he could under the circumstances. In his thirty-eight-hundred-foot apartment of four bedrooms and five bathrooms, one room had been reserved as a den, complete with a polished cherry wood desk, matching credenza and a series of cherry bookshelves. Perched on top of the desk was a nearly unused Apple Macintosh computer.

Roman sat back in his over-padded leather chair and depressed the power button. In less than a minute the screen came to life as the processor booted up. Roman could count on one hand the amount of hours he had spent on the computer. Making the adjustment to this new age of technology had been hard for him.

While the Internet was still in its infancy, the World Wide Web was growing exponentially every day. Email was replacing paper letters at a rapid rate and Internet searches had surpassed Yellow Page inquiries for the first time since the first directory was released eighty years ago. Companies like Ebay, Yahoo and Google were springing up from all corners of the tech sector as the stock market tried to keep up its pace in an ever-evolving industry that was both experimental and virtual.

Roman clicked on the bright blue AOL icon, typed his username and password and waited for the program to load and connect him to the Internet. As the popular online community took over his desktop, a familiar voice sounded through the computer's speakers.

"You've got mail."

Roman clicked on the letter icon and read through the list of incoming messages that dated back three months.

The first was from America Online welcoming him to the service. He had not signed up himself. A computer "nerd," as he called him, had come in and set up the system, dial-up modem and the online account.

The second was from an advertisement for Flowers.com, an automated florist, and the last email came from a man claiming to be the defecting prince of a Nigerian monarch who was wanting to hide thirty million dollars in a U.S. bank. And, for Roman's troubles, he was willing to grant half the sum.

Roman then clicked on the Internet browser function and typed a search query for *Zoë Greene.*

The search cue took a few minutes to load but when it finished it was almost seventy pages long. The first, much to his dismay, was the article that had appeared that morning in *The Observer.*

Strange Bedfellows.

The text that followed was a repeat of the tawdry article that had accompanied the pictures of Zoë and himself. At the bottom of the page was a link highlighted in royal blue. It had been installed as a footnote, trying in some feeble attempt to give credibility to the piece. *Mob-boss.com* seemed to blink as Roman clicked on it and the screen changed to one of a black background and gray-toned pictures that were arranged in a pyramid with his picture at the top. Below it were pictures of his captains and below that even more of the soldiers, some of whom were either dead, in prison or both.

He shook his head as he typed in *Evangeline's.* Ten pages of results appeared, most of which were listings in directories like the Yellow Pages and Zagat's restaurant reviews. He read through each appraisal like it was appearing for the first time in the *Times* or the

Post. Most were complimentary and the ones that weren't could only complain about the price. "You get what you pay for asshole," he whispered aloud.

As Roman turned off the computer, he reached up to the wall and pulled a framed cloth display that held his Purple Heart medal. He laid it on the desk as he caressed the metal edges and remembered.

Roman had adapted to Vietnam better than most where the terrain was rough and the jungles were bug infested. When the air wasn't blistering with heat, the days were filled with rain. Regardless, he had fulfilled his duties to the best of his abilities and was relied upon by those who commanded him. After his third tour, a stray bullet lodged itself into his right thigh. The injury earned him a Purple Heart, the rank of sergeant and got him assigned to the prestigious Air Cav unit, a modern day version of the historical mounted infantry. Instead of Thoroughbreds and Arabians, the soldiers rode the great new horse built of aluminum and titanium, the Bell turbine-powered UH-1 helicopter, otherwise known as the Huey.

The members of the Air Cav lived a notch above everyone else with better tents, better food and better beer. They were always awarded longer R & R's and partied like there was no tomorrow, because life at the sixteenth parallel meant this was a daily possibility.

Besides the flight crew, Roman had five men in his squad. His top three were a group of guys who had grown up, enlisted and served together since their first day of basic. They were from upstate Pennsylvania and admired Roman because he was from the city, the only city anyone in a two hundred mile radius recognized. The fourth man in the squad was a young hotshot redneck from Tallahassee, Florida named Brian Futch. He was a high school dropout that knew everything and nothing. PFC Futch was the major focus of the issues Roman had to deal with on a daily basis. He always wore a cowboy hat, listened to twangy country music and had a strong aversion to those of color.

The fifth man of the close unit was a thin black medic named Horace Greene. Most on the all-white team resisted Horace at first. The Army had been heavily integrated since a higher percentage of black and Hispanic Americans had been successfully drafted than in previous wars. While segregation was the norm, the powers that be were on a mission to change the racial makeup of its squads and end the dispersion that had been created because of it.

Futch led the charge against their medic while the three from Pennsylvania rationalized that many squads didn't even have a medic and that they should have been happy with what they had. Roman stayed silent, having been brought up to distrust black men in general. He had seen what men of color had done during the riots of 1964 and he despised the darker areas of the city. When he was feeling too hot or too wet, Roman would often rationalize, "hey, at least we're not in Harlem." Even his father Ray Senior used to say that "Hitler went after the wrong race...the blacks were a scourge against mankind, a lesser people that were closer to animals than to good, hard working, civilized men like us."

After time though, Roman could see that Horace was different from his embedded precognition of what black America was to him. He had been trained as a nurse and continued his medical courses, becoming a corpsman and a corporal. He enunciated his words and was respectful of everyone else on the team, even when they were attacking his dignity as Futch often did. Roman also admired the fact that, despite his advanced training and nursing job back in the states, Horace still left his wife and enlisted on his own.

As for himself, Vietnam was not entirely of his own doing. Enlisting was not something Roman would have contemplated on his own. He had been drafted, drawing one of the unlucky numbers in the lottery. His parents had rejected the thought of their only child coming home in a rubber bag. Roman Senior paid the proper people and within twenty-four hours the young soldier-to-be had the option to get classified as a 4-F, a medical ranking that ensured his early dismissal.

Much to the dismay of his mother and the indignation of his father, Roman turned down their assistance, going forward with boot camp at Fort Dix, New Jersey and his first tour at the age of nineteen.

He had seen men come and go and had seen death and dismemberment at a rate that stretched his own comprehension. It was because of this that he kept to himself without getting close to any of the other soldiers, including those that had been assigned to him.

To Roman, Horace, with the obvious exception of his skin color, was white. He talked like a Caucasian, better even, than most did back home in the tri-state area. He was educated and had an attractive white wife. Other squads, he rationalized, were dealing with real problems like heroin, civilian abuse and something they were calling "post traumatic stress disorder." *Yes*, Roman thought to himself, *things could be worse.*

Futch didn't care about any of that but seethed at the idea of Horace's white wife. "Mixed marriages are an abomination to God, Jesus and all humans, white and black," he would say. "Inter-raciality," a word he had a hard time pronouncing, "is an idea conceived by those damn hippies who spit on us when we go home for leave." Despite the hostility though, Horace would still pass around his one picture of his wife, his Melanie. Most of the team took a look. A few made comments. Futch would pass it on like a florist holding a wilted flower.

At the end of the day though, Horace Greene was part of the team and, like it or not, the rest of the squad had to accept it. As time passed Roman was forced to spend more time with him. He was different, Roman continued to rationalize. He was, after all, the first black Jew that he had ever met. When Roman was shot, Horace was there with a field dressing and a quick shot of morphine to squelch the pain, doing all of it in the open with the constant risk of being shot himself by the same Vietcong that were hell-bent on killing Americans, even those who were wearing the bright red cross on their shoulder. After that, Roman treated the man differently. They had bonded in a way only soldiers could, ignoring each other's skin color. And that is why, with the new rank he was granted, Roman decided to make a stand.

Futch had increased his taunting of Horace to a point that the rest of the unit was starting to grow weary of the same old comments and jabs by the bitter cowboy. What had been ignored was now front and center. Then one day Horace had had enough.

"What's your problem man?" Horace yelled.

"Only one, boy!" Futch answered, poking the medic in the center of his chest.

"I've put up with your shit for the last time!" he advised as Futch reached for Horace's left breast pocket and pulled out the one picture the medic had of his wife Melanie.

"Give that back to me."

"God hates this you know. The jungle should mix in the jungle," Futch replied as Horace reached for the picture. As he did, Futch lifted the picture above the shorter man's head like a taunting child in a schoolyard, tripping Horace to the muddy ground before throwing the picture into a puddle next to the downed man's head. As Horace reached for the picture, Futch stepped on the man's head, pushing it deeper into the mud.

"Stop it. That's enough!" Roman yelled, coming up behind Futch.

"Oh come on Roman. He had it coming," the bully rationalized as Roman jabbed his knuckles into the standing man's left eye. Futch fell like a rock as Roman put his muddy boot square on the man's chest.

"You fuck with the man one more time and I'll end you myself," Roman warned as he reached down and pulled Horace to his feet as the others in the squad looked at Futch with a disapproving stare. Then, the four standing men helped the medic by cleaning the mud off his uniform. One of the boys from Pennsylvania even took the picture and wiped it clean before handing it back to the medic. From then on Horace walked a little taller and the cowboy from Florida kept to himself. For the next few months the squad seemed to get along until one hot November night.

During the patrols, Futch had always stayed back, leaving the aggressive assaults to the boys from Pennsylvania. His favorite phrase was "gotcha back bro!" which meant that Brian Futch was going to surround himself with as many bullet-absorbing bodies as possible. Roman had noticed this and began putting the Florida native on point, a position that required Futch to walk a hundred meters ahead of the rest in a mixed recon-decoy stance. As an act of rebellion, the chastised solder would purposely make as much noise as possible, kicking the loose brush and downed limbs at his feet. During one patrol, Futch's loud gait drew the fire of a lost Vietcong soldier detachment. The men dove into a small crater that had been created by a downed tree. As the unit watched from behind the large horizontal tree trunk, Horace spotted the straggling enemies. Before Roman could dispatch one of his Pennsylvania sharpshooters, Futch grabbed a grenade from his vest, pulled the pin and threw it towards the sound of the Vietcong. Instead of traveling in the direction

Futch intended, the grenade bounced back into the five-meter hole. The device had been set with a two second delay, which is exactly what was going through Horace Green's mind when he dove atop the small bomb, absorbing the majority of the blast. He was killed instantly.

It took Roman three days to write the letter that would eventually inform Horace's widow Melanie Greene how her courageous husband had died. He rewrote the letter several times, trying to include every detail and convey the message that he and the others in the squad were alive because of Horace's actions. It was the hardest three days of his life in the jungle and possibly the most strenuous in his entire life. Roman traveled home to Brooklyn for the funeral where he presented Melanie with a folded flag and the last of Horace's personal belongings, vowing to do what he could to repay the woman for her loss, a loss that had saved his own life and the lives of others.

Chapter 16

3:13 AM
68 hours, 47 minutes left

It didn't take long before the animals of the night discovered the remains of Andrew Schultze. He had been left in the open and between the raccoons, wharf rats and a hungry fox, small pieces of flesh had been picked away from the body. It wasn't until a pack of street dogs started fighting over the bloody hulk that the partially clothed cadaver was dragged into the highway.

When a New Jersey State Trooper drove down the Meadowlands off ramp from I-95, he could see that the scene was far from under control. A group of cars had pulled to the side of the road and a citizen had placed an erratic line of red road flares that would have confused even the soberest of drivers. A small crowd had gathered and most were pointing frantically. In the middle of the road was a bloody mass that was the subject of a fight between two street dogs that were biting and gnawing at the remains.

"Please do something!" an excited woman yelled from the side of the road. The call had originally been dispatched as a traffic accident, specifying a vehicle verses a pedestrian. It was quickly becoming obvious though that this was not going to be like anything he had ever handled before. After radioing his station, the trooper donned his hat and approached the crowd.

"Please officer, do something!" the woman repeated.

"What happened?" the trooper asked as ten of the bystanders answered at once.

"One at a time please," he reasoned.

"I was coming down off the ramp when I saw this pack of dogs fighting over what I thought was a deer," a uniformed utility worker explained. "I stopped short here and from the pack, a German Shepherd I think, ran out in front of my headlights gripping a man's hand in his mouth. That's when I knew this ain't no deer."

With that the trooper left the crowd as some tried to follow.

"Please, wait by the side of the road," he ordered. As he got closer he watched as two street dogs had regained gnawing at what appeared to be a human torso. A few feet away, the victim's head wrapped with duct tape, lay with assorted pieces of flesh in between. The trooper picked up one of the road flares and waved it at the dogs.

"Scram!" he yelled as the dogs ran in opposite directions.

"Jesus!" he whispered to himself as he grabbed for the shoulder-mounted microphone that was connected to the radio on his belt.

"642 – Newark. We've got a vehicular homicide. Send me some backup and make it quick."

Thirty minutes later an entire four-acre area surrounding the Meadowlands off ramp had been cordoned off with a yellow police line. Units from animal control had arrived and captured two of the dogs for forensic evidence. Eight state patrol cars surrounded the scene as forensic technicians combed the area for more evidence.

The case had been turned over to the New Jersey State Police Investigations Branch, whose priority was to get a statement from the first trooper on the scene.

"The victim was dismembered and positioned in the middle of the apron of this off ramp over here," the trooper explained, pointing over to the overpass.

"Did any of the motorists indicate that they may have seen anyone placing the body before the pack of dogs took over?"

"I really didn't get a chance to question anyone sir. My priority was to secure the scene," he replied as he spotted something on the concrete overpass a hundred feet away.

"No, you're right. Good…"

"Sir," the trooper interrupted. "When did we get traffic cameras down here?"

"Holy shit," the investigator remarked as the two looked up at a new surveillance system that displayed its readiness with a small red light mounted to its top.

"You need to come work with us," the investigator told him as one of the crime scene techs approached.

"Detective, I think I found something."

"Well, what is it?" the investigator asked.

"A recent cigarette butt, and judging by how wet it is, my bet is that we've got some DNA to go on."

Chapter 17

8:18 AM
63 hours, 42 minutes left

With a few keystrokes, DSS Special Agent Joel Kenyon entered his user name and password into the mainframe system of EPIC, the El Paso Intelligence Center for Organized Crime. As per the court ordered federal wiretap and surveillance warrant, all phone calls, Internet traffic, emails and hard mail were to be searched and detailed records made of their content. The electronic evidence had been piped directly through a specially placed T-1 line that was installed at 450 Park Avenue North, Unit Nine, the home of Roman Sabarese. While Evangeline's was protected as a diplomatic annex to the Italian Consulate, the target himself and his personal residence were not.

As Kenyon's computer advanced through the protection faults and firewall safeguards, lines of file icons appeared on both sides of the screen. On the left were the file directories for the different electronic transcript abstracts marked *Hard-line Phone, Mobile Phone, Internet, Email* and a special cache labeled *Interior Residential Surveillance.* On the right were direct links to the actual digital files themselves including sound files of the actual calls and copies of the pages the target viewed on the Internet and his email traffic, both inbound and outbound. At the bottom of the list on the right side was an icon for the hard mail. A block had been installed at the midtown branch of the United States Post Office to intercept and hold all mail addressed to the target. Turnaround was mandated at no more than three hours, which meant that an agent had to wait for the mail to be dispatched, collect it, return to the main FBI office at the uptown Federal Building, open the mail, scan each document including the envelope, reseal the articles and return the items before they were set for delivery the same day. Most days, the mail had been easy to transfix to the digital format. Some were not. All it took was a bound circular or magazine and an FBI evidence tech could be tied up for two and a half of the three hours the warrant had allowed for the search. On more than one occasion, dark tinted sedans with federal plates raced through the streets of the city with their lights and sirens blaring just so the target's mail could be copied and returned in time.

Kenyon started by clicking on the icon that was shaped like a small globe and labeled *Internet Traffic.* Much to his surprise, the target's files were fairly shallow since the warrant had been issued twenty-six days before. Still, the agent opened each page and forwarded a copy to the case file that lived within the massive hard drive of the FBI's Organized Crime Unit for the Manhattan Field Office. The files were listed in reverse order and Kenyon smiled as he opened the first link that took him to the homepage for a website called *Mob-boss.com.* He thought it humorous that someone like Roman Sabarese would browse such a page. What was even stranger was that the target's picture was at the top, front and center, heading the hierarchy of what the site called *The Modern American Mafia.* Below the Sabarese photo was an organizational chart of the regular suspects, many of whom had just pranced through the front door of Evangeline's.

The next page on the list was a bit more perplexing. The target's search for Zoë Greene led him to over three hundred pages ranging from the official site for her television series *The Prosecutor*, to the homepage for a tabloid called *The Observer*.

While entertaining, the target's Internet traffic revealed nothing of importance. Kenyon closed the window and opened the icon labeled *Telephonic Traffic*. Each call that was made with Roman Sabarese's cell phone was cataloged with either the number dialed or the number calling, both party's exact locations, the duration of the call and a sound file of the actual call itself. Fortunately for the senior agent, the elaborated software allowed him to assign actual names to the numbers on the screen, making it easier in the long run for the one analyzing the information to see who was talking to whom.

Most of the calls made from his cell phone were to Nello Falcone, the restaurant's manager. The second highest frequency of calls had been made to Max Weintraub, another of the government's targets, and the third was to the restaurant Evangeline's. Kenyon continued to scroll down and that's when he saw it.

"What do we have here?" he asked aloud.

Seven calls had been made to a yet-unidentified number. Kenyon did a cut and paste of the number and inserted the digits into the FBI's mobile phone database. After digesting the request, the number came back as a recent account with the carrier Tri State Cellular. The account was for unlimited cell phone usage and an added Blackberry data plan. The notes stated that it was set up as a comp account for marketing and promotion although no name was given.

Seven calls? he thought to himself.

His next query was to Tri State Cellular with a formal FBI request for the user's name and physical address. Those requests, while common, usually took a day or two to process. For now the calls would be labeled as an *Undetermined Person of Interest.*

"Hey Joel! Look at this!" his DSS intern called out.

"What is it?" Kenyon replied as he logged out of the EPIC system.

"Looks like another sit-down."

Kenyon joined the young agent at the window. "Good job! These are the rest of the Sabarese captains."

"Jesus..."

"Spazio, Geraldi, Vincente and Minardi. That's all of them."

"What do you think they're up to?"

"I don't know but I'd give anything to be a fly on the wall right now."

Chapter 18

8:30 AM
63 hours, 30 minutes left

It was the second such meeting in as many days. The remaining four members representing the hierarchy of the Sabarese family sat seemingly transfixed over table 21.

Roman had kept them waiting for a reason. He knew that the time alone would increase their anxiety about a meeting that had been called so abruptly.

As Devon approached the table, Gino Spazio lifted his head to order.

"Vodka on the rocks retard," Gino spouted disrespectfully as the mentally challenged dishwasher took his order *and* his insult.

Gino ran the thirty-four different sanitation contracts in New York and New Jersey. Of the Sabarese captains, Gino was the only one who lived in Jersey, residing in the trendy community of Englewood.

The next to order was Salvador Vincente. Sal was over the eighteen Sabarese- controlled pawnshops that fronted as the largest loan sharking operation in the state.

"Dewar's, straight up Devon," Sal said as the dishwasher wrote.

"A beer for me, son," the next captain requested.

Tony Minardi was responsible for managing the New York Longshoremen and transportation unions. He had been fighting an outraged stomach ulcer and thus ordered a beer.

The last was Peter "Petie" Geraldi. Petie was the family's top earner and derived profits from the sale of everything from unstamped cigarettes and alcohol to forty-six escort agencies and massage parlors.

"Scotch Devon, nice 'n clean."

"Nice 'n clean," he repeated with a simple smile.

As Roman entered the dining room, Gino started to slide out of the booth.

"No Gino, don't get up," Roman said, grabbing a wooden chair from an adjacent table. He slid it over to face the four who remained seated in the round booth.

"What gives boss?" Tony asked as Devon came in from behind him with the drinks.

"What does Mr. Roman want?"

"Coffee, please Devon, thanks."

"You're probably wondering why I asked you here," Roman said.

"It did cross my mind," Tony replied as the rest chuckled.

"Things are changing gentlemen. I don't have to tell you that. Our ranks have been weakened significantly and those of us that are left have been placed under a microscope. Senior and I have spent hours deliberating and what we've come up with is the following," Roman paused as two of the four took a sip of their drinks. "This is a good thing, and in the end, it will mean more money in each of your pockets."

"You want us to stand out Roman?" Petie asked. He had always been the perceptive one. It was a trait that Senior had admired about the sixty-one year old man since he became a *made* man in the early seventies.

"I do Petie."

"Jesus," Gino said. "Who's gonna…"

"Watch out for you?" Roman guessed. "You can do what you've always done – watch out for each other. That will never change. What will differ from the past is our involvement."

"But why?" Gino asked.

"Consider this the big billiard break Gino. It's a matter of survival for us all" Roman detailed.

"I still don't get it."

"The way it is now, they go after one, they go after us all," Petie tried to explain. "What Roman's doing is to create four different organizations, each one separate from the other. Cutting the strings that bind us makes it harder for the G to scoop us with one net."

"There's the matter of the buyout. Senior established all of your respective operations and we need to be paid back," Roman said.

"Jesus, here it comes…" Gino commented under his breath.

"Gino!" Petie rebuked.

"Yeah Gino, chill the fuck out and show some respect," Sal said.

"It's okay. I understand your apprehension. This will be fair. Max and I have gone over the numbers. The bottom line is that you will be paying your next six months in advance, as in by the end of the year."

"But Roman, how will we know what we'll make by June?"

"It's based on your last six Gino."

"That's fair," Petie said, setting the tone.

"And that's it, we're on our own?" Tony replied.

"Done deal," Roman reiterated.

"Six months in two days? Roman, I don't know if…" Gino hemmed.

"Gino, your share is six-fifty large."

"I don't know. It's still a big chunk to come up with in a short time."

"I can cover it and you can work for me Gino," Tony said.

"No thanks big guy. I'll make it work."

"Petie, you're at three point four five"

"Ouch!" Gino said.

"Tony, one point four."

"That's fair Roman."

"And Sal, two point three."

"More than fair boss," Sal replied.

"By the end of the year gentlemen," Roman reiterated. "And there is one more thing. It's kind of personal. As I'm sure you're aware, this rag that calls itself *The Observer* has a cover story with yours truly."

"I saw that crap," Sal said with vigor. "You want me to send a message?"

"No Sal. It's best ignored. I've got a bigger problem. The night that this story hit the street, our friend and former valued employee of the restaurant, Zoë Greene, disappeared and hasn't been seen since."

"You sure she's not laid up at your place?" Gino said with a smirk as everyone else at the table looked at him with a stern face. "Sorry Roman."

"You might want to show some respect. This can't be easy for the man," Sal reiterated.

"I said I'm sorry. I'm Sooooorry! Jeez…" Gino replied with shrugged shoulders.

"Let's keep our eye on the ball people. She's a responsible kid and not one to just run off. It's my fear that something's happened to her. There's a lot of sickos in this town."

"You got that right Roman," Petie agreed. "Let me put my ear to the ground and see what I can find out."

"Thanks Petie," Roman said.

"I'll see what I can do…and sorry for the crack, really," Gino answered without making eye contact with Roman.

"Call me or Nello with anything…and I mean anything."

Chapter 19

12:32 PM
59 hours, 28 minutes left

Special Agent Joel Kenyon stood at the hostess's podium next to his wife Tessa as they waited for a table.

"Welcome to Evangeline's. I understand this is a special anniversary for the two of you?"

"Yes," Kenyon replied. "Thanks for reserving a table on such short notice."

"It's our pleasure, and it helps that it's for a lunch seating. Our dinner schedule is booked all the way through March."

"Wow! We're not from around here. We wanted to experience a Times Square New Year and figured this was the best time to do it."

"Well, I hope you enjoy your stay. I will have to put you on the ground, our balcony is completely full."

"That'll be fine," Mrs. Kenyon added as the three walked over to table 18. "Thanks, this'll be great."

"Jess will be with you in a minute."

"Very nice Agent Kenyon," his wife said with a devilish smile.

As he hung his jacket on the back of his chair, Tessa pulled a digital camera from her purse.

"You're going to owe me big for this," she said, laying the camera on the tabletop.

"What time is your hearing?" he asked, looking down at his watch.

"3:00 PM at the federal courthouse on Foley Square."

"Good, just relax and have fun. Lunch is on the Bureau."

"It had better be. We can't afford this."

Kenyon's wife was still getting used to life in Manhattan. She had graduated from George Washington Law School two years before and had secured a lucrative position with a Wall Street securities firm in their legal department. Still, Manhattan was far more expensive than their last home in Virginia where the couple and their two children had been living for the previous six years.

The lunch was as much a treat as it was a part of her husband's assignment.

"Hi, I'm Jess. Can I go over the lunch specials with you?"

"Sure," she replied with an eager smile.

The Australian waitress repeated her rehearsed list of tantalizing items as the couple smiled and listened intently.

"We need a second, but first can you take our picture?" Kenyon's wife asked.

"Sure," Jess answered, taking the camera as the agent and his wife posed next to each other. With the snap of a strobe flash, the two reclaimed their seats and Jess handed the camera back to him. He set it back on the table, leaving the power button in the *on* position. A small red LED light stayed illuminated as Kenyon positioned the lens toward table 21, just eight feet away. Had this been a regular digital camera, a device known for depleting its battery power rapidly, the camera would have been dead by the end of the first course. But, this was no ordinary camera.

With the flick of a switch, Joel activated the video mode and parabolic microphone function. As the two took their time ordering and then eating, the camera continued to record everything that was in its field of view.

* * *

Roman sat seated in his round booth sipping some coffee and going over a vendor proposal for a new line of flavored rums. As he scanned the different line items with a pair of reading glasses perched on the end of his nose, Bones came over to his table and slid in from the opposite side.

"You tired?" Roman asked.

"Three cups of coffee to get me out of bed."

"How did it go?"

"It's done," Bones replied.

"Good. Anything we can use?"

"Nothing. This girl just vanished."

"I've got someone else we need to look at…" Roman said as Jess interrupted him mid-sentence.

"Roman, we've got a problem with the credit card machine."

"What is it? Where is Nello?"

"He said to get you," she insisted.

"Shit. Hold that thought. I'll be back in a few," Roman said as Bones grabbed two breadsticks that sat in a basket on the table. As soon as Roman rounded the corner and entered the loud confines of the kitchen, Jess confronted him, whispering into his ear.

"The guy at 18 is up to something," she said as Roman's eyebrows raised.

"What gives?"

"He's got a camera. Looks like the same one my sister's got, but the damn thing weighs a ton. There's no way it's for real."

"How heavy?"

"Two kilos."

"Jesus."

"And it's pointed at your table with the power light on."

"QT baby girl," Roman said with an index finger to his lips.

"What?" she said smiling.

Roman returned to his table as Bones wiped the breadcrumbs from his mouth.

"Mind if I order lunch?" Bones asked.

"Another time, okay?"

"Okay…"

"On second thought, go ahead, order away," Roman said, getting the waitress's attention.

"Jess, get Bones set up. It's on me."

"Hey, thanks Roman," Bones said as he ordered three full courses. "I'm famished."

"Ya think?" Jess replied sarcastically.

"I've got to fix the credit card reader. Enjoy brother."

Thirty seconds later, Bones' phone rang.

"Yeah?"

"Hey, it's me," Roman said. "Don't talk to anyone. Eat your meal, enjoy yourself, but only open your mouth to put food in it."

"Okay?" Bones questioned.

"The guy sitting two tables away with the pretty little wife is a federal agent and he's got a camera pointed in your direction."

Bones didn't need any prompting to subdue his table manners. He had spent the last thirteen years in crowded prison mess halls eating tasteless food in record time. Jess brought his three courses at once with a record ticket time. Instead of a salad he had opted for a bowl of the house special, the pasta fazool, a creamy soup with fresh white beans, shredded garlic, cheese, and a rich tomato broth. Like a vacuum, Bones sucked down every last drop.

His next target was a plate of lobster ravioli with a vibrant red sauce. For this, Bones tucked a white napkin into the nape of his neck. As he began to shovel, pieces of food started to color the white fabric like paint on an abstract artist's fresh canvas.

Two tables over, Joel looked over at his wife who had stopped eating.

"You okay?"

"The guy over there acts like he's never seen food before," Tessa Kenyon replied as Bones stopped and looked in their direction.

"So where you guys from?" he asked with his mouth half full of food.

"Virginia," Kenyon answered.

"Bet it's nice down there."

"We like it," his wife said with an awkward smile.

"This your first time?"

"Excuse me?"

"To the city. Is this your first time?" Bones repeated.

"No…but our first time here."

"You like it so far?"

"This salad is to die for," she replied with a smile.

"Lady, you don't know the half of it."

Chapter 20

11:06 PM
48 hours, 54 minutes left

Feeling confident and enthusiastic about their new assignment, Nello and Bones entered the condemned building on Chauncey Street in Bedford Stuyvesant where the acrid smell of crack and cigarette smoke filled the air. On the floor, microbags, candy wrappers and human feces covered the painted concrete. In desolate corners, vagrants and the drug addicted homeless huddled in the heatless building, clinging to rotten mattresses and shreds of weathered cardboard.

Nello and Bones watched their steps as they made their way through the chaos. Each one carried a metal gallon jug of liquid that sloshed about as they walked. In the back of the ground floor standing next to a cinderblock stairwell, a young girl in her twenties stood. She had unkempt blond hair and a prominent nose ring, was dressed in torn jeans and a soiled *'N Sync* tee shirt, and had been waiting for them.

"He be all the way upstairs," she announced with a manufactured urban accent.

"What's he wearing?" Bones asked.

"Red and white striped shirt. He's got some girl wit' him and I think he gonna hurt her real bad."

"Here," Bones said, spotting her two crisp one hundred dollar bills. "Don't spend it all in one place."

"Thanks. Maybe we can party later? I still owe you that discount," she offered.

"Probably not sweetheart. Some other time," Bones said.

"If anyone asks…" Nello added.

"You was da' biggest, baddest niggas I eva' seen," she said with a smile.

"Hey, start getting all these people out of here. Tell them the cops are on the way," Nello instructed as he started up the four flights of stairs before looking back at his partner.

"You take her to meet your mom yet?"

"Hey smartass, after thirteen years, pussy is pussy," Bones replied as a pale scream echoed from the top floor. As they hustled faster the chunky ex-con was reminded how much he hated steps. He was out of shape and his two hundred and seventy-five pound frame held him back as his heart pumped through his chest in an effort to keep up. With Zoë on his mind, Nello, who weighed just as much, raced up the stairs half a flight ahead of his partner who was panting uncontrollably.

"Stop for a second," Bones pleaded.

"We got to get you in shape man," Nello said looking back at Bones who was resting, hunched over on his knees.

"Oh yeah, fuck you," Bones said as another scream came from the top.

"Come on man. What if that's Zoë? One more flight."

As the two crested the last step on the fourth floor they could see what all the commotion was about. A small fire in a distant corner filled the large room with a dull orange glow. In the opposite corner a bearded man with long curly hair was kicking a naked girl. She had olive skin and her hair was straight with jet-black locks. She was clinging to a dirty blanket and tried her best to dodge the blows the man was sending her way. A surge of energy flowed through Nello's veins as he raced over to the two.

"You must be Young Jesus," Nello said.

"Hey, what the..." the man said as Nello punched him square in the throat.

After absorbing the full shock, the man fell backwards onto the hard cluttered floor, grabbing his crushed windpipe. Nello looked over at the young woman who was, as he could now see, no woman at all. She was a young girl and not Zoë.

"Oh my god!" Nello gasped.

"What is it?" Bones asked, coming in from behind.

"This kid can't be more then twelve."

"What's your name sweetheart?" Bones asked, taking off his jacket to cover her.

"Kayle..." she whimpered.

"Hey! She's mine. You can't..." the attacker said, scratching his words out as Bones stomped squarely onto his face with his size thirteen steel-toed boot.

"He said his name was Young Jesus. I just needed a place to stay."

"How old are you honey?" Nello asked.

"Fourteen. I want to go home."

"You will. How long have you been here?" Bones asked.

"A day and a half," she replied as Nello pulled a picture of Zoë out of his pocket.

"Have you seen this girl?"

"No, it's dark in here. He wouldn't let me move around much. I'm cold and hungry."

"Where are you from Kayle?" Bones asked.

"Kearny, across the river. My mom and I had a fight and I hitchhiked into the city."

"Kayle, we're gonna get you out of here but you have to make me a promise you will never pull a stunt like this again," Nello said as he collected her clothes that were strewn about.

"I'm so sorry..."

"Get dressed sweetheart," Bones said.

"What the fuck do we do now?" Nello whispered to his partner.

"One of us has to get her downstairs. There's a hot dog vendor on the street. Put some food in her stomach and get her ass in a cab as soon as possible. I'll take care of things up here, and Nello, on your way down, make sure all these misfits know the cops are coming. I want this building vacant - *except for one*," Bones instructed.

As Nello made his way down the stairs with the girl, his partner went to work on Young Jesus.

"You with us baby Jesus?" Bones asked, slapping the man in the face.

"Can't breath..." he grunted with a sharp rasp.

"Sorry to hear it. Look, we're missing a friend of ours. She's twenty-five or so, half black...goes by the name Zoë."

The man, with his head on the dirty floor, leaned it to the side as he looked Bones in the eye. With blood streaming from his mouth and like a man with one sentence left before death he pronounced, "I don't fuck niggers."

"Wow, a purist. I don't believe you," Bones said as he emptied the first gallon from one of the jugs over the man. Young Jesus started to gasp as he could detect the bitter smell as it soaked into his clothes and skin.

"Can't breath."

"Relax Jesus, it's just acetone."

The man spit and grunted, trying to clear his mouth and throat of the volatile liquid.

"Now, tell me, where's Zoë?"

"Don't know no Z…"

Bones kicked the man in the gut as he bent down to question him one more time, knowing that time was starting to run out.

"Jesus, what's the oldest girl you ever fucked?"

"Fifteen."

"Okay, that's good enough for me. Acetone evaporates pretty quickly. Can't have that," Bones said as he started to pour the second metal jug over Young Jesus and then dripped a thin trail towards the burning flame in the opposite corner of the room. As he did, the fumes reached the fire before the liquid did and a bright blue flame rose up and shot across the room towards the man who couldn't help but remain prone on the floor. As the bolt of blue light approached his limp frame, the fumes from the first gallon that had soaked into his clothes, clear through to his skin, ignited.

Bones made his way down the stairs as Young Jesus' throat opened up one last time to expel a series of ear shattering screams. On the way down the four flights, he tried to balance his heavy frame as he looked through each flight to make sure everyone was gone. As he exited the front entrance to the sidewalk, Nello had just hailed a cab and the girl was devouring a hot dog, some street meat for the ride home.

"Look Mohamed, here's a benny. Take the kid over to Jersey. She'll give you the address on the way. Do it right and do it now and you can keep the change. Got it?"

"Yes sir!" the cabbie replied as a bright orange glow consumed the sky above and the top floor of the building became fully involved with fire.

Chapter 21

11:54 PM
48 hours, 6 minutes left

FDNY Engine Company 124 and Ladder Company 111 knew they would need help when they headed down Malcolm X Boulevard towards Chauncey Street. The entire top floor of the condemned building was fully involved with a brilliant orange glow that lit up the night. Four alarms later, two city blocks were occupied with more fire apparatuses, police cars and detectives from the 79th Precinct who were on the ground asking questions and working hand-in-hand with the New York State Fire Marshall's Office. The scene looked more like a discothèque with the swatches of red and white light that flashed across the brick fascia of all the surrounding buildings. In the bitter cold, ice had started to form at the junctions of the fire hoses where small leaks had turned solid. Closer to the buildings, an adjacent fire hydrant looked more like an elaborate ice sculpture as the frozen liquid around it grew with each passing hour.

The precinct detectives considered this a tremendous opportunity to round up some of the wanted criminals in the area that had evaded them for so long. The inhabitants of this sliver of the underworld were now lined up across the street from the burning building, huddled under blankets and trying to stay warm. Since many of them were addicted to drugs, dealt them or both, a pragmatic plan had to be put into place to detain, segregate and question all of those who called this crack den home. Fortunately, most of the displaced had outstanding warrants and those that didn't possessed enough residue or related paraphernalia to justify an arrest.

On the sidewalk a news crew from NBC 4, standing over snaking fire hoses, caught most of the action along with the four precinct transport vans that loaded up the survivors. "At least one is believed dead after a devastating fire claimed this abandoned building on Chauncey Street." And the words "a tenement, some call a crack den..." became the sound bite for the evening as the battle to bring the fire under control continued into the early morning hours.

Back at the 79th Precinct house, the collection of eighteen sat on long benches where some were still shaking from transient wave of DTs. All were covered with blankets and sipped warm coffee from white Styrofoam cups while they awaited their turn to be debriefed. Two hours later, one of the building's prominent residents, a blond twenty year old with low self-esteem and poor impulse control named Marnie was spilling her guts.

"You told us the guys you saw were two large framed black dudes," the lead detective reminded her.

"That's what I seen," Marnie lied.

"So why is everyone else telling us about two white guys that sound more like a pair of fat guidos than gang bangers. And who owns an old black Ford Bronco?"

"I didn't see no Bronco," she replied, clinging to her urban dialect.

"But since your story stands out, it's my bet you know something. Do I need to remind you that besides your thirty-eight arrests for solicitation, you've got an outstanding warrant from Jersey for aggravated battery?"

"That's bullshit!" she yelled, sounding more Anglo with every word.

"You tried to stab your pimp didn't you?"

"I can't go back there. He'll kill me."

"Well, tell us what we want to know and we'll cut you loose. Forget we even saw your face."

"Yeah Marnie, what happens in Jersey gets to stay in Jersey," came a softer voice from the lead's partner, a policewoman in her early thirties.

"I think they call him Bones or T-bone…something like that. I think he just got out o' the joint cause he did me like that, you know. But hey, this dude's connected so you can't let no one know it be me who dropped da bomb on them. I'll end up in the East River you know!"

"Them?" the lead asked.

"There was two of them, like I said before. I never seen the other guy. He was a fat Italian too. They paid me two hundred bucks for info 'bout this dude Young Jesus."

"Young Jesus was in the building?"

"Yeah, he was on the top story wit' some black haired chick. The Bones dude was looking for some bitch named Zoë. Ain't nobody eva look fo' me," she said holding her head low. "They thought the chick with the black hair was this Zoë."

"Was it?"

"No. The chick was young. The other fat guy brought her down and bought her a hot dog and put her ass in a cab."

"Where to?"

"Don't know"

"Okay Marnie."

"I really don't know what they was driving."

"It's okay," the lead said, content with her testimony. "We've got cameras, four on that street alone. We'll find 'em. So where do you think Young Jesus is?"

"Oh, he didn't go very far," she said with a smile.

"What do you mean?"

"He burned up."

"You sure?"

"I heard the screams. That shit musta hurt."

"Those two dudes do this? Burn him up?"

"That was the point I guess. That's why you gots to protect me. These guys don't mess around."

"We'll watch your back. You've got to sign a statement though," the policewoman replied.

Chapter 22

Thursday 3:18 AM
44 hours, 42 minutes left

Bones stood at the back of his black Ford Bronco. He smoked a cigarette, taking deep drags as he looked up at the sign of the building he was parked in front of as Nello's cream-colored Cadillac Seville pulled up behind. In bold, twenty-foot-high letters the billboard read *The Jersey Meat Company* and had been a sore point in his personal history.

"Something tells me you're gonna enjoy this more than me," Nello said to his partner.

They both stood and looked up at the three-story building that was centrally located in the heart of the Meatpacking District. It looked like most of the other buildings in the area with the exception of having a paneled glass exterior over the top two floors. This had been created to let natural light in to the building and heat during the winter months. Bones finished his cigarette before tossing the butt to the ground. It had been thirteen long years since he was sent away for price fixing and money laundering, two charges that had come from the direct testimony of the owners of The Jersey Meat Company, the very place they were now parked in front of. The owners had been as equally involved as Bones was but had turned state's evidence to avoid any prison time. Their pleas ensured them a sentence that was reduced to probation while at the same time sent Bones to Terre Haute Prison for the better part of thirteen years, a place he vowed to never return to at any cost.

"Let's do this," Bones said as Nello popped the trunk of his Cadillac.

"Hey Walter," Nello said as the metal lid flew up revealing a short, fat man that had been tied and bound with several bands of gray duct tape.

Walter Gibbons was a regular at Evangeline's. He had always hung out at the bar, ordered the same drink, a vodka and cranberry, that he sipped while he consumed his weekly plate of veal parmigiana. He would take his time, eating small bites as he gawked at the young ladies in the restaurant and watched his favorite team the Knicks on an oversized TV that was mounted on the back wall behind the bar.

There were times that he would make small talk with Nello who had the habit of leaning against the bar a few stools away as he oversaw the workings of the restaurant. Nello didn't mind, despite the fact that he knew Walter's colorful history.

In 1982, the then forty-two year old shoe salesman from Queens had been arrested and charged with capital sexual battery or CSB. His suspected rape never made it to trial as the star witness, the victim, a twenty-two year old student from NYU, committed suicide the day before jury selection.

Between 1984 and 1989 there were six different investigations of rape and sexual battery but nothing ever stuck. All six alleged victims were NYU students. It wasn't until 1991 that Walter was indicted by a grand jury on three counts of CSB against another NYU student that had been held captive in his basement for a week. As part of a plea bargain, the then fifty-two year old served three years at Attica Prison in upstate New York.

"Where's Zoë?" Nello asked.

"Umm mmm mm," Walter grunted through the three bands of gray duct tape that covered his mouth.

"Oops. I'm sorry Walter," Bones apologized as Nello looked around the front of the building.

"All clear," he said as the two pulled Walter from the tight confines of the trunk. The prisoner had his hands secured from behind with two plastic wire ties, nylon strips that were used by electricians to bind large bundles of cable. They walked him to the front door of the large agora warehouse that Bones had jimmied open earlier. Once inside, Bones ripped the tape from Walter's mouth.

"What the fuck?! Nello! You know me!" Walter pleaded.

"Yeah, I know you Walter. Where is Zoë?"

"I ain't got no idea…didn't know she was missing."

"Bullshit. I see the way you look at her Walter…everytime she comes into the restaurant. You got short eyes you piece of shit and I got the Internet. You ever look yourself up on da Internet Walter?" Nello asked.

"Please, I did my time."

"Yes, sure you did. Three years for rape and kidnapping," Nello said as Bones looked away with disgust. *This guy does three years for raping and torturing a girl while I got thirteen for playing with numbers*, Bones thought to himself.

"You like the NYU girls. Zoë was an NYU girl, but you know that."

"Oh my God! Please don't kill me!" Walter pleaded as the stench of diarrhea filled his pants.

"Jesus, Walter," Nello said as both men looked away to grab a fresh breath. "Kill you? Shit, you're one of my best customers. You tip well, don't spill your food on the bar...why would I want to kill you?"

"I didn't do it!" he pleaded.

"Hang him up," Nello ordered as he began losing patience.

Bones took Walter up a steel gantry that led to the processing portion of the facility.

"What are we doing?" the scared man asked, trembling as he spoke.

"Tell us what we want to know and you can go home," Bones reminded him.

"Yeah Walter...I'll even throw in a veal parm to go!" Nello said with a laugh.

Bones took a heavy half-inch length of chain and wrapped it around Walter's chest and under his restrained arms. Then, while holding the man with one hand, he grabbed a six-inch iron hook that was dangling above from an overhead electric winch, the likes of which hung from a heavy trolley system that had the ability to slide back and forth on an I-beam that was attached to the ceiling. Once hooked, Bones grabbed a switchbox that was hanging from the electric winch and depressed a blue one-inch diameter button that had an *up* arrow painted over it.

"Oh my God, please don't!" Walter cried as the winch lifted the chubby man off his feet. As he floated in the air, Bones pushed him and the trolley-mounted winch slid across the I-beam. Walter sailed across the open space like an angel at a school play. As the momentum slowed, Bones gave him another nudge that sent him just above the hungry mouth of the processor.

"So tell me Walter, you ever jerk-off to the thought of Zoë?" Nello asked from the ground as he waited. Walter continued to sob uncontrollably.

Bones hit the next button on the switchbox, a red one with a *down* arrow painted over it. The electric motor clicked into motion as the chain grappled through the round gears and Walter lowered closer to the processor.

"Shit Nello!" Bones yelled down after realizing they had forgotten something. "Turn the damn thing on."

"Where?" Nello yelled back, looking at a control panel that was mounted to the face of the massive machine on the ground level.

"The green button on the side – right in front of you," Bones yelled, pointing down at his partner.

As Nello depressed a two-inch green button a large motor started to wind up, sounding more like a jet on the tarmac at JFK than an oversized meat grinder.

"Okay Walter, one more time," Bones yelled over the sound of the machine. "Where is Zoë?"

"I swear, I don't know!"

Bones bumped the red button of the dangling switchbox one more time as Walter dropped a few inches.

"Come on Walter, this isn't going to be pretty," Nello yelled. "Tell us what we want to know and we can go back to being friends."

"I swear to God…please! Why would I hurt Zoë? I love her!"

Nello and Bones stopped for a second and looked at each other.

"What did you say?" Bones asked.

"I love Zoë! I think about her every day. I watch her show and I dream about being with her."

"Where you got her man?" Bones asked.

"I ain't got her Nello!" Walter cried as Bones hit the red button again.

"Okay, okay!"

"What Walter, where is she?" Nello yelled up.

"I don't know, but I jerked off during her last episode," Walter yelled with a shamed look on his face.

"Oh Walter," Nello yelled.

Bones hit the red button for the last time with a look of frustration. Walter squirreled on the chain like a wild animal that had been caught in a snare. The frightened man descended, screaming, trying to contort his body away from the funnel-like mouth of the machine he was drifting down towards.

"Okay! I jerked off twice. TWICE! That's it!" Walter yelled before coming in contact with the shredding blades that sucked the penny loafers from his feet before the churning blades bit into his flesh. Walter screamed one last time before falling unconscious. His limp body dropped slowly, inch by inch, before being devoured by the processor that deposited the finished product in a large stainless steel vat below.

Bones and Nello made their way out of the front as the chains entered the shredding blades of the processor. Massive sparks filled the large open warehouse and illuminated the tall glass panels that made up the top two stories of the building as the rest of Walter was reduced to a lesser state.

Chapter 23

5:40 AM
42 hours, 20 minutes left

A tinge of smoke lingered through the open warehouse that was The Jersey Meat Company. It was a secondary effect from the hundred pounds of tempered steel chain that had come in contact with the machine designed to shred a substance that was much more digestible. It had been a linear reaction after that, like an erect line of dominoes falling one after the other. The smoke triggered the fire alarm that awoke the building's owner, the officers from the 1st Precinct and the FDNY from Station Ten. As the machine continued to devour everything in its funnel-like mouth, the chains bound to the shredding blades and shut it down, but only after the expensive damage had been done. When The Jersey Meat Company owners entered the building with the fire department at their side, it only took them a few minutes to find the source of the smoke. At first they were drawn to the stainless steel vat that sat below the massive machine that had small trails of acrid smoke flowing from its vents. The men shook their heads as they looked at the vat that was filled with ninety pounds of multicolored textural meat. After climbing the gantry, what they found would change the entire tone of the evening.

Twenty minutes later, with the fire trucks gone and the parking lot filled with blue and white police cruisers and crime scene units, Fitz looked over the processor from the gantry. Inside the funnel mouth was the top half of Walter Gibbons' torso, the part that was left after the chains fouled the machine. He sat frozen and devoid of any color as though all the blood had been sucked out of his body. His eyes were open and his head was leaned back, indicating that he might have been conscious when his terror occurred. *Or for part of it at least*, Fitz thought.

"What do you think the motive was?" a subordinate officer asked.

"Revenge? Walter's got a shady past. Rape, torture, he's a real sick bastard this one is, I mean was," Fitz said, correcting himself.

"You think a woman did this?"

"It's a nice thought, but no. This guy had to be pretty strong. My guess is we're dealing with at least two perps here," the senior detective rationalized as a CSU photographer came in behind him, snapping shots of Walter's upper remains.

Fitz took his time. While he would hand this over to two detectives in his unit, he wanted to make sure he had a grasp of what had happened long before they were called. This was going to be one of those bizarre cases that cops loved talking about around the poker table or during a 4th of July barbeque. Most of the issues his office dealt with were written off as personal petty problems or PPP. "Why can't we all just get along," the detectives used to repeat almost comically, recalling the iconic words from Los Angeles beating victim Rodney King. The cases they were used to had been simple thefts, assaults, an occasional rape and once a month, a murder that was usually the result of two people that knew each other well and had social differences that spiraled out of control. It wasn't like the weekly thought-provoking episodes of *Law and Order*. Although many of the episodes were based on real cases, one season usually represented years of real life, twisted tales that had made legends out of the people on the streets of the city and the cops that investigated them.

Thirty minutes had elapsed and Fitz was outside. *The electrical smoke was like none other*, he concluded as it had caused a headache and inspired a wave of nausea that he didn't have the patience for.

"Do we have any tire marks?" he asked one of the CSU techs.

"None. They weren't in a hurry when it was time to leave. There is a fresh oil stain over here," the tech explained, pointing to a small puddle of black oil in the pavement. "The vehicle they were driving was not a late model. Besides that, we've been all over the place with a fine-toothed comb. There are no surveillance cameras pointed towards the lot, but we can still look over the traffic units to see who came and went."

"So I guess this belongs to someone from your crew?" Fitz asked, bending over to look at a cigarette butt.

"Now, how did we miss that?" the tech questioned as he pulled a small evidence bag from his toolbox.

"Get it to the lab and see if you can get any DNA off the tip," Fitz ordered as the tech picked up the spent cigarette with a pair of tweezers.

Chapter 24

8:10 AM
39 hours, 50 minutes left

It was a stark contrast from the harsh cold outside as Roman entered the building with Max at his side. Warm air filled the corridors that were decorated with cinder blocks painted a glossy gray and steel, double-locked doors. Danbury Prison was an oasis in a field of white snow. It was encapsulated with a twelve-foot-high chain link fence that was crowned with three rolls of razor sharp concertina wire. Danbury, while not the highly publicized super-max, was still a medium security facility and ranked at the top of the federal herd. This was to be his third visit to the facility since his father was arrested on Thanksgiving Day over a month before. This was just one of the many reminders of what was to be the eventuality of their *thing*, the family, and the people who had grappled with its defiant lifestyle for so many years. As bad as it was, prison was one of the favorable outcomes. It was, as some had rationalized, better than a defection living as a rat in a cage, looking over one's shoulder at every turn, working a nothing job under the constant, nagging supervision of some witness protection bureaucrat. Prison was also better than death, although some would have debated the idea. *Could there be another option? Had I created one?* Roman thought to himself. After all, he hadn't asked for any of this; he never bargained for the risk to his freedom, his life and certainly not the risk to Zoë's life. *Zoë,* he thought, *what have they done?*

A mechanism closed the steel door behind him. Like a train with two heavy freight cars slamming together, the shock could be felt through the painted concrete floor, through his shoes and up his spine. Roman was having a hard time getting used to the heavy metallic clink that had sounded at his back, reminding him that he was now on the inside.

For all the speculation and wild conjecture that was married to an even bigger reputation, Roman Sabarese had never been incarcerated. He had only been arrested once and that was temporary with him not even making it to the back of the waiting squad car before an intervention stopped the process. Still, the iron, concrete and sterile gray, glossy paint on the block walls was a reminder, making it all rather real of what his father was dealing with on a daily basis. It was what he had been able to avoid and what his father hadn't.

Max waited behind as Roman advanced another hundred feet to the family room where he took a seat. Furniture made of steel and Formica occupied the nearly thousand square foot space. In one corner a plastic playhouse was erected and was surrounded by broken and abused toys. His family hadn't been the only one affected by an incarceration.

Ten minutes later another clink shook the floor followed by the sliding action of the population door opening as Ray Senior entered the room. He walked slowly into the room like a man who counted his steps. He was already starting to lose some of his hair, not that he had a lot to begin with. To his son, he looked thinner and his expensive wire-rimmed bifocals had been replaced with thick, prison issued black-rimmed glasses. His skin looked like that of a white resin, transparent and wrinkled past capacity. It had only been two weeks since his last visit and yet he could see the marked deterioration in his father's eyes. While most prisoners gained weight, Senior had already lost sixteen pounds since that fateful Thanksgiving Day.

"Did you get the magazines I sent you?" he asked.

"You know I can't get things like that. Didn't you read the list?" Senior replied with an agitated tone.

"Yeah I read the list. I just thought…"

"What? That I had something worked out? They move these guys around too much now. It's almost impossible. You make a connection in here with a guard and then, poof! He's gone. It ain't like the ole' days kid," Senior replied, pointing to the camera mounted in the ceiling next to a TV that was broadcasting an interview with former White House intern Monica Lewinski. "Fucking cameras everywhere. Can't take a shit without them makin' a movie."

"I know it's tough. I'm sorry."

"It ain't your fault," his father said in a softer tone as he leaned over and kissed his son's forehead.

"Hey, you been watching this crap?" Roman asked, pointing up to a TV. "They're reliving the whole thing just in time for next year's election."

"Yeah," Senior said, cracking a smile. "He should have cum in the girl's mouth. If I was the president, you bet…right down her fucking throat so she couldn't spit it out. Instead this redneck blows his business all over her pretty blue dress," Senior said, pausing, "okay, I would have done that too."

"This place is starting to warp your head Pop."

"You think?" Senior replied with cresting eyebrows.

"What did they do with your food?" Roman asked, trying to change the subject.

"Oh God, they totally fucked it up. Tried to get the doc to say I needed more tomatoes 'cuz I had low acid and shit. It backfired. That little Jew prick," Senior said, stopping for a second before whispering. "Where's Max?"

"It's okay Pop, he's in the other room."

"That little Jew prick, wouldn't you know, put me on a salt restrictive diet. Canned ravioli and tater tots and no salt."

"I'll get Max to see about getting you a second opinion."

"You do that. In the meantime what I'd really kill for is some fried calamari from the restaurant and some real cheese for Christ's sake. None of this imitation crap they feed us," Senior objected before saying softly, "some buffalo mozzarella with sliced tomatoes."

"Caprese salad?" Roman offered.

"Yeah, caprese salad," he replied with a smile. "Okay, now I'm gonna drive myself crazy. It's all I think about. Most of these guys obsess about women. They jerk off in the cell. They jerk off in the shower. You gotta watch your step around here. Everybody's business all over the place. It don't matta. No fucking respect."

Roman sat silent.

"I just miss my food son."

"I know Pop. I get it. Look, I wanted to ask you…how far do you think these Russians would go…you know…to bring us down?"

"I really don't think they got the stugots."

"I think it's more than balls Pop. Something strange is going on."

"What? Has anyone made a move…on you?"

"No, nothing like that. It is getting more serious though. I think they took Zoë."

"What? That little nigger girl – the hostess?"

"Pop!" Roman objected.

"I'm sorry, African American. I seen her on TV the other night. She's pretty good."

"We can't find her."

"And why you lookin'?"

"She came into the restaurant last Monday and disappeared into thin air. Nobody..."

"Why you lookin'?" his father asked again, this time with a sterner tone.

"Pop," Roman replied as his father looked down at the floor.

"You never did have any control over those colored girls."

"It's not like that."

"The hell it ain't."

"No control Pop? No control over this? That was a long time ago and you had no right. You destroyed something in me. Did you know that?"

"It had to be done. I did it for you. That shit was going to fuck up your whole life."

"Well, in response to that, here's what I'm doing for you. I've assembled all the captains."

"Good. Take the initiative. That's what I want to hear."

"No Pop. I've asked them to stand out."

"What?! Are you crazy? You want to ruin *us*...me?"

"Look at you," Roman responded, pointing around at all the steel doors and monitoring cameras. "Look at this. Is this how you envisioned it all ending up?"

"We can beat this son! My attorney says..."

"I know what he says. I was there, remember? But maybe we won't. Maybe we shouldn't. Really, that indictment weighed two pounds...I know, I held it. All it takes is one of those charges to stick and you go away for life. So...what are you gonna do? Cut a deal? Go become a ward of the witness protection program?

Please...you wouldn't make it a month...they'd have you working as a bag boy in some grocery store in Ohio or Minnesota."

"Do you know how hard I've worked for this? For you and your mother, and God bless him, your brother? Do you know?" Senior yelled. "Fuck it! I'll call Big John myself and tell him there ain't no deal. Reverse the whole thing. You can't do this to me."

"The hell I can't. By the time they approve the visit – *if* they approve it – the deal will be done," Roman finished as the two sat quietly before Senior looked up at his son.

"I did it for you son."

"Good bye Pop," Roman said abruptly as he stood and walked to the door, hitting a flat red button on the wall that sounded a buzzer in the guard's office.

"I did it for you!" Senior yelled as the door opened. Like a freed captive, Roman squeezed through the metal frame without waiting for it to slide completely open.

"What is it?" Max asked as Roman met him in the foyer.

"It's not him. He didn't take Zoë."

"So what the hell was going on in there? I could hear your dad yelling all the way into the reception area."

"Oh nothing."

"He didn't know did he?"

"What?"

"Your plan to make the captains stand out. You never talked to him...did you..."

"Max..."

"You said that you both discussed this. I backed you up because you said the plan was consensual."

"It is what it is Max. It's survival."

Chapter 25

9:51 AM
38 hours, 9 minutes left

Nello and Bones walked down the dingy hall that led to Ariel Zillo's apartment off Francis Lewis Boulevard in Queens. For Bones, a day didn't pass that he hadn't missed the action of "the good ole days," as they called them. For him the action wasn't the payment; not that he wasn't paid and paid well for his deeds. He had been a valued member of Ray Senior's close circle and had done things he couldn't or didn't want to remember. Still, he was an addict, just like all the rest, except for him the drug was adrenaline and his dealer lived within his own brain.

As the two made their way towards the apartment at the end of the hall, their steps were camouflaged by the common noises found in any rundown urban apartment building. Crying babies that belonged to parents too young to absorb the responsibility associated with infants, youth who couldn't provide for themselves much less a child that was now wailing away in one of the tenements. They walked twenty steps further and an elderly man popped his head into the hall, restrained in place by an oxygen cannula that was feeding his nostrils. He looked down the hall and then back, seeing the two men walking in his direction. They were both dressed in black great coats, wore black sunglasses and leather gloves. *They were either cops or crooks, neither and both,* he thought before pulling his head back into his bug-infested cave of an apartment like a turtle retreating back into its shell. This apartment was his meager existence and his recollection of the two men that were assaulting his hallway would be erased as soon as he threw the four deadbolts that secured his front door to its steel frame.

In the open they kept walking, maintaining a common, non-descript appearance. It was what they were striving for; that and as many witnesses as possible. Unlike TV and movies, they knew that a witness's account was the most unreliable in the evidence pool. This fact was compounded by the multiple witnesses that would invariably give a different skewed account of what they saw, or in reality, what they *thought* they saw. The buffet of statements that would remain would be as different as the people giving them, which was much to the benefit of Nello and Bones since neither wanted to join Ray Sabarese Senior or enjoy any of his new accommodations.

The two stopped at a partially opened door. Behind it was a small box fan; the type that was tall and thin and had a plastic or metal grate on either side, except this one lacked any such protection as its sharp blade spun freely. It was sucking air through the door that was propped open, four inches past the jam, held in place by a flimsy security chain that was attached at eye level. Bones took a pair of common electrical dikes out of his coat pocket and snipped the chain first. Then, as though it had been planned, he cut the cord to the fan. The dikes were insulated with heavy rubber handles which protected the olive-skinned Italian as a small spark popped at the site and the blades wound down to a stop.

"What the…" came a voice from inside the dark apartment. As Nello felt the man approach the inside of the door, he kicked the swinging metal panel with a sharp jab. The door flew inward, striking Ariel in the forehead. The man fell backwards to the concrete floor as his world went dark.

* * *

Ten minutes later, the twenty-four year old suspected rapist sat in one of four wooden chairs that surrounded a Formica kitchen table. As he regained consciousness, he realized his situation had changed for the worse. Ariel was secured to the chair with wide bands of gray duct tape and his hands were taped to the table in front of him with his arms outstretched and his palms facing up. He looked more like a representation of Da Vinci's *Anatomical Man*, a specimen or a guinea pig secured to a dissecting pallet in a high school biology class. *Da Vinci would have liked duct tape*, Nello thought to himself.

Bones loved duct tape also, like a cat loved milk. By the end of Ariel's ordeal, he would use three full rolls. And he didn't buy the cheap stuff. Bones preferred the industrial grade brands that were manufactured to meet the specifications of their original design, which was to secure large tunnels of heating and cooling ductwork. It was the good stuff with extra adhesive and a fibrous mesh that made it extra strong.

Tears started to pool in the deep sockets of Ariel's sunken eyes as he grunted against the bands of tape that wrapped around the back of his head and ran through the corners of his unshaven mouth.

"Relax Ariel," Nello said in a calm voice.

""UMM…Umm," he grunted, trying to breathe through his congested nostrils.

"What's the matter big boy? You gotta cold?" Bones asked as Ariel nodded yes.

"We got a little problem Ariel," Nello said. "We're missing a friend of ours. A pretty, well-kept little thing. Just your type."

"We're told you're the one to talk to. That maybe you can shed some light on where our friend might be," Bones added.

Ariel didn't move. He just looked at Nello with eyes that resembled saucers filled with bloodshot milk. Sweat started to form and stand on his brow as the two men could hear the air move more rapidly through his constricted nasal passages.

"You breathin' okay man?" Bones asked with a sense of manufactured compassion.

Ariel started to tremble as the pooling tears flowed down his face.

"Our friend's name is Zoë Green. She's biracial, black and white, mid-twenties, last seen at Evangeline's in Tribeca."

Ariel tried to grunt through the duct tape as Nello cut the bands free from his mouth.

"I don't know who you are talking about," Ariel said frantically.

"You mean you don't know her, or you don't know where she is?" Nello said sternly as Bones removed the rusty pair of electrical dikes from his great coat for the second time.

"I mean, yeah, I know her," he replied nodding down at a rumpled copy of *The Observer* with the color pictures of Zoë and Roman on the front page.

"Okay, so you know her," Bones said.

"Yeah man, everyone knows her," he relayed nervously.

"So where's she at?" Bones asked.

"I don't know," he said, trembling.

"That's a problem," Nello said as Bones took his cue. With a swift movement he dissected Ariel's left thumb from the rest of his hand. As their prisoner screamed, Nello shoved a rag into his mouth, muffling the sound. Still, Ariel continued to scream on the inside like a battalion of fire truck sirens and he started to lose consciousness again.

"Stay with us man, come on..." Nello said, slapping his grimy, stubble-covered cheek. Ariel snapped to, opening his eyes wide again.

"What about the others? What can you tell us about them?" Nello asked as he moved the man's amputated thumb to the other side of the table.

"Can I get that back?" Ariel asked.

"We'll see. Tell us about the others," Bones ordered.

"The first was named Risa. She was jogging to her gym."

"You watched her for a while, didn't you," Nello offered.

"Yes. I can't help it man! I'm tri-polar and shit."

"I think it's bipolar Ariel, but that's okay. I understand. There are a few things I can't help either," Nello said with a chuckle.

"What are you going to with me?" he asked.

"That depends," Bones said. "Where's Zoë?"

"I don't know. I never..." Ariel shouted as Bones interrupted him by snipping off his right thumb thereby causing a small spurt of blood from the man's newly formed nub. Nello, ready for the scream, shoved the rag back into the prisoner's foul mouth as his head went limp.

"Bump him," Nello ordered as Bones pulled an EpiPen out of his other coat pocket. This was a pre-filled syringe of epinephrine, a synthetic form of adrenalin. This was a necessary ingredient to combat the psychological shock Ariel had succumbed to. Bones popped the plastic cap and jabbed the short prong-style needle into Ariel's leg. Immediately the clear liquid drug flowed into the man's subcutaneous tissues. It only took a few seconds for the agent to work as Ariel awoke, talking in rhymes.

"I don't know where she be man," he insisted.

"Tell me about the other girls," Nello asked.

"There was Angel. She worked at the public defender's office."

"And how did you meet her?" Bones asked, knowing the answer.

"She was workin' on a beatin' case I had a few years ago."

"And how did they do for you?" Nello asked.

"Got me off," he said, cracking a small smile before looking down at his hands and the two thumbs that were lying unnaturally apart from them.

"Okay Ariel, we're getting the point. What did you do with Angel?"

"I couldn't help myself!" he insisted again.

"And Zoë?" Nello asked.

"No!" he yelled. "I swear."

Nello looked over at Bones who was by now realizing that this was a dead end as he opened the apartment's tight wood-framed window.

"What are you doing?" Ariel asked as a flood of cold air entered the small room.

"The world a favor," Nello answered.

*　　　*　　　*

The foot traffic was sparse as the howl of the falling man approached the stone and concrete sidewalk six stories below. While New Yorkers were hard to shock, a crowd soon formed at the mess that was made. A collage of wood, human flesh, bone and gray duct tape made up a pile of artistic debris as a pool of blood grew larger at the base with each passing second.

Chapter 26

4:08 PM
31 hours, 52 minutes left

Blue and white police cruisers surrounded the area at Pier A in fashionable Wagner Park. A three-inch stream of yellow police line tape secured a five-acre area along the Hudson River. On the water and fifty feet off the concrete and stone shore, an NYPD forty-foot Grumman police boat maneuvered, thrusting its twin diesels against the current. On the aft deck two police divers suited up and prepared to search the icy waters for clues.

From the south a blue and white NYPD helicopter came in low, creating a thousand ripples in the brown water below. With the skill of a veteran, the pilot hovered low and close to the scene. Inside the chopper, a CSU tech snapped photos as other police observers also looked for clues.

On the outer band of parked vehicles, a string of news vans from the major media outlets idled. A farm of extended towers rose into the air supporting microwave antennas that beamed edited packages from the scene. Sharply dressed correspondents from the different networks made their claim on strategic spots around the site, each one with a clear backdrop of what had transpired, a backdrop that *had* to include the police cars, flashing lights, a hovering helicopter, and floating in the water, a woman's body covered with a yellow tarp.

Bodies floated down the Hudson on a regular basis, some were suicides, some were murders and some were simple accidents. Most didn't get the media coverage that this one did and for one explicit reason: the epicenter of the world's biggest party was just days away and this made for great television. And for this reason, it was also a great source of pressure for the detectives of the 1st Precinct to identify the victim and, if any, the cause of the unintended death. Timing was paramount to defuse the media storm of speculation that oftentimes turned into a skewed perception that could have disastrous results, especially during such a concentrated event.

As the supervising detective, Fitz climbed down onto some breakwater rocks to get a better look. Cold water splashed up through the huge boulders as one of the techs lifted the corner of the tarp. The body had drifted from the north and got tangled in a floating sheet of ice that was clinging to the bulkhead of an adjacent concrete seawall. Now it just floated like a patch of limp seaweed, rolling with the small swells.

"How long has she been dead?" Fitz asked the on-scene medical examiner.

"Hard to tell. Once we get her out of the water I can do a quick probe of her liver."

By probing the liver and taking its temperature, a technician could tell with an accuracy of plus or minus thirty minutes, the victim's time of death or TOD. It was a complex calculation that had to include the water's temperature, which at times made it impossible to determine. Water cooled a body four times faster than air and since the Hudson was close to freezing, it wasn't uncommon to see a floating body cooled completely through with a temperature matching the ambient level of the water it was immersed in.

"Any signs of foul play?"

"Oh, they didn't tell you? We've got a bullet wound to the right temple. Besides that, her head has been beating against these rocks for a while now. It's going to be hard to separate the two," the medical examiner explained.

"I don't have to tell you that the timing couldn't be any worse for this kind of thing. I need an ID as soon as possible. Let's pray she's local and not a tourist. If we're not careful this whole case could blowup in our faces," Fitz explained as he looked closer.

She was a light-skinned black woman and judging from the skin on her extremities, he determined her age to be between twenty and thirty-five.

"Detective…" one of the correspondents yelled down to the rocks. "What can you tell us about the victim?"

"I'll have a statement for the media within the hour. Now please stay behind the yellow line…"

"I'm sorry Captain," one of the uniformed officers apologized as he came up behind the questioning reporter.

"Behind the line," Fitz repeated, pointing to the back of the lot. "This is turning in to a circus."

"I'll get you something soon," the medical examiner replied.

"Please."

* * *

At the end of the long cherry-wood bar, Nello sipped on a cup of coffee while the bartender flipped through the channels searching for a good game to broadcast on the oversized wall-mounted TV. It was the lull before the dinner rush, a chance for everyone to recharge their batteries, consume some caffeine, and prepare for the surge that would start by 6:00 PM and extend deep into the long night. As the screen's picture changed from channel to channel, a quick glimpse of a crowded police scene flashed as a blond reporter began her story.

"A woman's body was found…" the words continued as the bartender advanced the channel again.

"Stop!" Nello yelled. "Go back one channel."

As the station changed, Nello sat back onto one of the stools with his jaw hung low. With a myriad of police cars and a hovering helicopter, a local NBC news reporter stood front and center holding the familiar multicolored peacock embossed microphone.

"This is Amanda Russell, News Four, on the shores of the Hudson in Wagner Park where police from the 1st Precinct are investigating a floating body," the reporter said as the wind blew through her hair.

"Get Roman!" Nello yelled.

"Police have no clues at this time," the attractive reporter continued.

"What is it?" Roman asked, bursting into the bar area.

"Look at this," Nello replied as the scene on the TV changed to a suit-clad black man with a badge hanging from his breast pocket.

"At 3:47 PM officers from the 1st Precinct received a call that a woman was found floating facedown in front of Wagner Park, about a mile north of the Battery. The victim has not yet been identified," a spokesman from the NYPD said as a ticker spelling his name, *Stanley Fitzgerald, Detective Captain, 1st Precinct*, flashed at the bottom of the screen. "This is what we do know. She was a black woman in her twenties or early thirties and she appears to have been in the water for at least eight hours. One bullet wound to her right temple has been discovered. We will be able to give an update after the medical examiner completes his post mortem. Anyone with any information is encouraged to contact the 1st Precinct. Your identity will be kept anonymous."

Roman stood in shock.

"Don't jump to conclusions," Nello said. "Harlem is just up the river. This kind of thing happens all the time."

"So why all the cameras? Did you see that scene?" Roman replied. "That's the crime scene of a celebrity."

"What celebrity?" the bartender asked.

"Shut up and get back to work," Nello barked as the man grabbed a rag and started cleaning a set of beer mugs.

"Oh my God," Roman said softly.

"Relax, it's probably…"

"You don't know…" Roman said as his cell phone rang.

"Yeah?"

"Roman, it's Melanie…oh my God! Are you watching this?" she cried.

"I just caught it. Has anyone tried to call you?"

"The phone's been silent all day."

"That's a good sign. Stay put, let me see what I can find out."

"Roman?" she replied, "what have we done?"

"Stay put and don't call anyone."

Chapter 27

5:35 PM
30 hours, 25 minutes left

The traditional brick and stone building that was the 1st Precinct house was busier than usual. With less than two days until the new millennium the city's hysteria was close to peaking. Assaults had doubled and crimes against property were statistically the worst in fifteen years. At the morning briefing the duty sergeant compared it to a New Orleans Mardi Gras, a Rio Carnival, the 4th of July, Christmas, and or course, New Year's Eve all rolled into one twelve-hour period. Combined with the threat of a worldwide computer shutdown, the men and women of the 1st were on edge.

Roman Sabarese walked the busy sidewalk towards the precinct house. Every fifth or sixth pedestrian turned back to look at him as though this was Hollywood and he were an A-lister himself. His profile had been featured on the front page of *The Observer* and every other underground newspaper that specialized in celebrity gossip. His image had also maintained a permanent place within the masthead of the popular mafia website, *Mob-boss.com*. If Roman was anything in the city, he was now one of its most mysterious celebrities. As he opened the heavy wooden door that separated the warm interior from the cold street below, the noise of the circus inside hit him, looking more like an agitated crowd at a heated boxing match. In one corner, a domestic dispute had erupted, taking two uniformed officers to keep the embattled couple apart. On the prisoner's bench sat five scantily dressed prostitutes, part of a street sweeping operation that was designed to better the city's appearance for the expected swarm of television cameras and attached media that would be bringing the new year ritual to the rest of the world. In addition, the ringing phones, crying babies, irate victims and a barking dog that was tied to the door of a holding cell, all made for a montage of sound that resembled a train wreck and not the peaceful order that the police department of New York City was supposed to project.

As Roman walked into the large foyer it seemed to cause a shockwave that transcended the entire room. One of the prostitutes noticed him first, tapping her "co-worker" on the shoulder while pointing at him, then another, and another until the clutter of selfish voices turned into a quieter blurry hush. And then the entire room went silent with the exception of one oblivious desk sergeant. As the house stood still in disbelief and with all eyes on him, Roman walked to the front desk, ignoring the recess he had caused. The sergeant behind the partition was deep in conversation with a victim on the phone and was oblivious to what was occurring around him.

"Ma'am, I told you, we don't have enough officers to look for your husband. I'm sure he'll show up soon…probably in a couple of days," the officer yelled back into the phone as he looked up, meeting Roman's stare.

"Oh my God!" he blurted out, dropping the phone. "Can I help you Mr. Roman…I mean, Mr. Sabarese sir…" he continued, tripping over his poorly placed words.

"Yes Sergeant, is Captain Fitzgerald available?"

"He's on three…Detective Bureau," he replied with eyes wide open.

"Thank you Sergeant."

As Roman made his way to the stairs, the paused chaos behind him resumed as though he had never been there. In the meantime, the duty officer must have called the third floor to warn them because as Roman crested the last step all eyes were again on him. This time it was a dozen plain-clothes cops that all had large side arms, some of which were belt clipped in heavy leather holsters while others wore theirs on the more traditional torso wrap with a gun under their armpit. Most of the men were in business attire with their shirt sleeves rolled up. A large fan circulated warm, moist air in the corner of the room. Most of the men had sweat stains from the perspiration. Despite the single digit temperatures outside, most of the building's heat accumulated at the third floor like a trap. While the rest of the building struggled to stay warm, the Detective Bureau maintained a constant ninety degrees, summer, winter or fall.

As Roman walked through the squad room, an instant path was cleared for him as though he was an un-bathed homeless man walking through a crowded sidewalk. The path led to a smoked glass door with the letters *Detective Captain Stanley Fitzgerald, Robbery Homicide*, painted neatly with gold leaf letters trimmed in glossy black pin stripping. Roman knocked on the door as it rattled with every rap.

"Come in Roman," Fitz yelled.

As the door opened, Roman saw a much older, weathered Fitz than he remembered. He reminded himself that it had been over twenty years since the two had seen each other.

"Of the things I thought I would see in this century, this wasn't one I saw coming. How have you been?" Fitz asked with an outstretched hand and a smile.

"Mind if I close the door?" Roman said as the two shook hands.

"What the hell…I'm going to have to see Internal Affairs after this anyway."

"Zoë Greene is missing," Roman announced.

"Missing? How Long?"

"The last time anyone saw her was Monday around 11:00 PM. I saw the dead girl down by the Battery on TV and…"

"Not her Roman. We'll announce in a few hours. Noonie Jackson was her name. A domestic gone bad up in Harlem. Oh it's nice to be down river…" Fitz said as Roman sat back in the chair, taking a deep sigh. "Have you filed a report?"

"Her mother hasn't. We're trying to keep this off the media radar."

"Got it."

"Can you help?" Roman asked as Fitz looked away for a minute.

"We go way back Roman and we've got our secrets."

"That we do. I need your help Fitz."

Roman pulled out a photocopied piece of paper and handed it across Fitz's cluttered desk. "I had my bartender pull this ticket. It's a copy of her credit card. The staff has been told that her money is no good in my place but I guess this guy was new and didn't know any better, and you know, he was just doing his job."

"Big items. A bottle of water and a Diet Coke," Fitz read.

"Zoë doesn't drink."

"Really?"

"She goes to clubs, likes to dance, that kind of thing but never caught the bug I guess."

"Sounds like someone else I know."

"Hey, not since Vietnam anyway."

"Roman, you're shattering the *Goodfellas* image all by yourself."

"If Hollywood only knew."

"Look…without filing an MPS…"

"MPS?" Roman asked, looking puzzled.

"Sorry, damned acronyms, missing persons statement," Fitz explained. "Without filing an MPS, there's not much the unit can do. Even if you did file a report, she's an adult and *officially* we're required to wait twenty-four hours before we can lift a finger."

"Officially?" Roman questioned.

"Officially," Fitz confirmed.

"I need your help," Roman admitted.

"Let me see what I can do. No promises."

"No expectations. I wrote her cell number and mine on the bottom of that credit card receipt."

"We've got some regular offenders who need to be checked on from time to time."

"Well, unofficially, you might have a few less."

Fitz's eyebrows rose as one of the detectives barged into the office.

"Sorry boss, I just got a call from the guys over at the 104th Precinct. Ariel Zillo was found this morning in a bloody pile on the sidewalk. Someone pushed him out a six story window."

"Take Peters and head over there. Let me know what you find out," Fitz said standing from his chair over Roman.

As the detective left the office, Fitz leaned over and shut the door.

"Look Roman…"

"Would it help if I told you he may have confessed to all four girls?" Roman explained as Fitz sat back in his leather chair and closed his eyes.

"All four?"

"All of 'em, but not Zoë."

"Anyone else we can stop looking for..."

"I've got a list."

"Oh sweet Jesus. This can't be happening," Fitz exclaimed as he buried his face in his hands. "I'm going to need to come by your restaurant."

"Come hungry...we can sit and talk."

"Probably not...thank you...but I think you understand."

"Sure."

"I will need to question your staff. Will that be a problem?"

"No of course not."

"And Melanie Greene. When is a good time?"

"You name it. We are at your disposal."

"This couldn't be happening at a worse time you know."

"I do and I can't begin to tell you how much I *appreciate* anything you can do."

"We'll see how much you appreciate me when I'm done."

* * *

"What was that about?" Detective Hector Alvarez asked as he slid into Fitz's office.

"It seems Roman's got a problem."

"And what's he expect? You go out on a limb for him?"

"That's where the fruit is Hector."

"So what's the deal?"

"You know that little black actress he's been hanging out with?"

"You mean banging," Hector said with a smile.

"Where did you hear that?"

"It's Zoë Greene. She's on every tabloid from here to Hollywood, and in all those pictures, Don Roman Sabarese is right next to her," Hector elaborated.

"Well, she's gone missing. Family says it's been around forty-eight hours."

"When was she seen last?"

"Monday evening, about 11:00 PM or so. And get this, she was at Evangeline's when she disappeared."

"No..." Hector said with a dropped jaw.

"Yes. Whoever did this, if there is a who, has got some great big balls."

"They file an MPS?"

"No, not yet. They don't want to alert the media."

"Yeah but..."

"Not yet Hector."

"So what is it with you two? Graft would be the obvious but I know you're not the type...so what gives?"

"He's the Teflon Don for a reason."

"Yeah, because he's smart."

"You ever wonder why every mid-level wise guy in this city wants him dead?"

"He's changing the game, isn't he..."

"You can always tell a lot about a man by the enemies he makes."

"So, you think the missing girl is related to all of this mob shit?"

"My first impression is no. What moron would risk the publicity?"

"Some of these guys aren't that smart Chief."

"If this was an abduction and the perp was a dumbass, Roman would have found them by now. He came to me because he's out of options."

"So what do we do now?"

"Let me poke around. How are things coming with linking Ariel Zillo to the Greenwich rapist case?"

"Guys over at the 104th Precinct say they found two thumbs in the apartment and a body, minus said thumbs, on the sidewalk. We both know Zillo's our man."

"Well, off the record, Roman's guys might have been the ones who did this."

"What? I've been on this case for six months. You telling me they solved this just like that?"

"Not before, shall we say, some manipulation."

"No shit…" Hector replied in disbelief.

"No Zoë, but you'll be happy to know he confessed to your four others."

"Mother Fuc…"

"Hey, QT Hector," Fitz admonished with an index finger to his lips.

"Yeah, sure. Can we give Roman anymore of our cases?"

"You'd like that, wouldn't you?" Fitz said with a chuckle.

"I'm just saying. I know of some pedophiles, a rapist and this guy who's banging my ex…they all might know where Miss Greene is…"

"I'll see what I can do…" Fitz concluded as Hector stood to leave the room.

"Hey Captain," Hector said as he turned back. "Anything Roman needs, you can count on me."

"Thanks Hector."

* * *

Roman despised all taxicabs, but this was the fastest way to get over to the East Village. The car smelled of sweat and the driver played a Middle Eastern song on the stereo that was unbalanced and over-based. To make matters worse, his driving style resembled an epileptic experiencing an active seizure. As the cab's brakes screeched to a stop, Roman pulled out a twenty to cover the eleven-dollar fare.

"Keep it," he instructed, bolting out the back door. As he stood onto the weathered sidewalk, he looked up at the tall four-story brownstone, checking the address with the quick note he had jotted down at the restaurant.

As Roman rang the bell Melanie opened the large wood and glass door, holding Trooper in her arm as she sobbed uncontrollably. Roman stepped in and held her tight.

"It's not her," he whispered into her ear.

"Oh thank you God!" she called out, dropping the cat to fend for himself. "I don't know how much more of this I can take."

"We're gonna find her."

"What about the police? I think it's time to do something."

"Already on it. I just left the 1st Precinct and talked to Stan Fitzgerald. He's gonna poke around and keep it all off the record," Roman told her as he looked over at a naked Christmas tree that stood over by the living room's fireplace. "Are you taking down the tree already?"

"We never decorate it. That's one of Zoë's traditions."

"You celebrate Christmas?" Roman realized with a question.

"Where can she be?" Melanie cried, sitting deeper into her couch as she ignored his question.

"I don't know, but we need to be prepared for anything," Roman replied as Zoë's kitten Trooper started to bite at his shoes.

"That damn cat is driving me crazy," Melanie conceded.

"I guess I could take him with me."

"Would you?"

"Sure. It's the least I can do," Roman said, picking up the crying kitten that started to purr immediately. "I have a feeling things are going to work out. Just keep your head up."

"I owe you so much Roman," Melanie said as she rested her head on his shoulder.

"And I you."

Chapter 28

5:40 PM
30 hours, 20 minutes left

Zoë was confined to a box about twenty-feet-long, ten-feet-wide and six-feet-tall. This was of her own doing. She went looking where she knew she shouldn't have and now the young girl was a captive of her own curiosity. It was dark, cold and worst of all damp. She had spent the latter part of the previous day and night curled up on the floor that was made up of crated wood that smelled of aged oak. An inch below her head under the suspended grate was a shallow puddle of stagnant water. The interior was lined with corrugated metal sheeting that smelled of rust. She had felt what she could last night with her hands but she was tired and the cold just made her crave sleep even more. Her cell phone provided enough dull light to see parts of the box. The Blackberry was the latest and greatest thing to hit the market that year. The "smart phone," as it was called, was a gift from one of the many celebrity boutiques she had frequented in recent years. Like free samples at a mall, this was a way for high-end manufacturers to get their products to market and in the hands of the trendsetters. Zoë always thought it was strange that the people who needed free stuff the least, received the most. In her perfect world these impromptu tents would be filled with the homeless, single mothers, and kids that were in foster care or orphanages. But, as she was learning, if the world was anything, it was far from perfect. Her good decisions though were coming from experience, and her experience from her bad decisions. Still, sitting in the confines of the box, she recounted the perfume, shoes, jeans, makeup, purses, sunglasses, keys to a high-performance rental car, diamond bracelet, earrings, watch, cardigan sweater, heavy leather jacket and Blackberry smart phone that were all free and yet also confined, unable to be seen by anyone who might replicate the style that had been chosen for her. Now though, the expensive accessories would be unable to be photographed by the lurking paparazzi and printed in the next day's gossip pages, and unable to provide free exposure for her benefactors.

It was all terribly ironic how she could eat, drink and party until her heart was content and do so without spending a dime, the whole time maintaining a reasonable level of selectivity. She had lived with her mother in their brownstone in the East Village. Melanie insisted that she wasn't going to pay rent and didn't take a dime for her keen management skills that had carved a successful career from nothing. Her expenses were limited to gifts for others, the ten percent she paid her West Coast uber-connected agent, taxes, and her generous gifts to the several local charities she had adopted over time, the dominating one being a charter school in Harlem. This frugality allowed her to invest a sizable portion of the one point seven million she was now earning each year, a sum that was just starting to escalate.

Zoë's plan was simple enough. She would work the trenches of TV and supporting roles for five or six years, bank her money, watch it grow, and then branch in to directing. With her own capital to invest, she could pick and choose her own projects. It was what she had been trained to do at New York University's film school, her alma mater. She had even gone so far as to start penning her own scripts. Her latest calculations revealed that, at a minimum, she was going to need ten million to create, produce and distribute her own feature motion picture.

She felt the dead Blackberry in her hand. Now it had the usefulness of a hockey puck. Zoë started to feel like an intellectual in a hunter-gatherer's world as she slipped it back in her purse. It was almost depleted when the ordeal had begun. The metal that surrounded her blocked any meaningful signal and with her several attempts to call out the battery soon beeped to a state of total exhaustion. She spent her remaining waking time working the locked door mechanism. It was like none she had ever seen, bulky with no palpable latch or release. The box that contained her was, she finally figured out, a walk-in freezer, abandoned and non-operational. It was cold enough already. The good news was that, judging from the light breeze flowing overhead, it was not an airtight cell.

On Monday night, after finishing off her special calamari, she had gone for a walk on the street. Some residual smoke from a burning vent fan in the kitchen had given her a slight headache and, for her, the cure was with some fresh air. That's when she saw it. A vendor at a street side newsstand, open late for the escalating tourist market, had just set out the next day's edition of *The Observer* bearing her picture next to Roman's and the tawdry headline, *Strange Bedfellows.* In tears and in shock, she walked four city blocks to her director Tim Bussy's apartment. He had always been a staple of compassion for her, a trait he'd acquired after losing his own love, a life partner named Allen to AIDS two years before.

It was there that she retreated, spent of the emotional energy she required to deal with such an unsettling blow. With her cell phone off and the blinds drawn, she buried her head in the pillow of a couch in his spare bedroom and disappeared. She was ashamed and distraught at what the paper had printed about her and a man she had only known to be kind and a true friend. For her, there were so many things to consider. It wasn't just herself she was concerned about; she was also haunted by what this new thread of publicity could do to Roman. If even a shred of the rumors about him were accurate, that he was the successor of his father's criminal empire, then this type of attention could be both disastrous and deadly for him, not to mention the repercussions that could fall on the restaurant.

After talking at length with Tim, she decided to go back to the restaurant and do some checking herself. In her heart, she didn't believe these things about him but it was the heart that forced her to know for sure.

On Wednesday she slipped into the restaurant's back door. It was easy for her to move through the place without being noticed. After all, she knew about every recess, crack and crevice in the place. Once inside she made her way to Roman's office where she retrieved a key that had always hung on a nail by the door. It was what would unlock the single door that led to the lower level, an area some had called the "sub-basement."

Most commercial buildings had a basement and Evangeline's was no exception. Theirs though, contained two separate restrooms and a mechanical area that housed the building's furnace, air conditioning system and electrical panels. In 1974, during an expansion phase of the New York Subway System, Ray Senior had paid off the contractors to dig a little deeper, excising a small cave-like enclave into the building's foundation. In time it was blocked off with concrete and stone and a stairway was constructed with its crest meeting a single door that remained locked in the women's restroom, one of the three rooms in the restaurant's basement.

On Wednesday, during a tourist surge that bolstered the normal lunch crowd, she entered the same women's restroom. After waiting for the lingering patrons to leave the usually congested area, she unlocked the door and descended down the long, dark carved-out stairwell. Thirty feet below, stairs met the concrete floor and a small caldron that housed a large discarded walk-in freezer.

It had been Ray Senior's original ambition twenty-five years before to create a secret area that could store files, pictures and the deepest secrets of the Sabarese organization. His only concern at the time was the moisture and mold that lived so far beneath the surface of the ground. Manhattan, after all, was an island, an island that was limited in its elevation, especially in the southern part of the city where the restaurant resided. It was two years after that in 1976, after the restaurant upgraded to a newer walk-in freezer, that Senior commissioned the old one be dismantled and walked down to the subterranean level piece by piece. It was then reconstructed and built into the cavernous wall where its airtight, water-resistant exterior could protect his important belongings and secrets. Ray Senior included this as one of his better ideas until the area experienced a series of high tides. The rising water coupled with a serious drainage problem meant that the area was prone to flood. This caused the metal freezer to start rusting uncontrollably.

After Roman took over the restaurant completely, Senior removed his belongings and his son assumed the space for his own causes.

Zoë rubbed her eyes which caused the cells in her cornea to create disturbing shapes, a phenomenon made worse by the total darkness she was immersed in. She kept her eyes open in an attempt to adjust the blackness to something viewable, but with the total absence of any light (and her pupils completely dilated) she was completely blind.

She should have at least called her mother. This was her real regret. Everything else had been unplanned. It was hard to face the woman. Her mother had worked so hard to build her career. Melanie had objected to her working at Evangeline's from the beginning and now that advice was proving to be true. *But then I would have never met Roman, another strong influence in my life,* she rationalized to herself.

Her next reaction was to feel the wall again. This time, she pledged, she wasn't going to miss an inch. Zoë glided her hands over the cold tin that made up the freezer's interior walls.

"Ouch!" she yelled out as her left ring finger came in contact with a sharp, jagged edge of metal. Warm blood ran down her finger as she stuck it in her mouth to stop the sudden flood of pain that shot down her hand. It was a small cut and it soon sealed itself as she nursed the wound with her tongue. *Enough with the walls,* she thought to herself as she stood on her toes, feeling the metal ceiling. It was just as uniform as its vertical counterpart. Because of the cluttered stuff in the freezer, she had to temper her steps while feeling again, inch by inch, putting her cut finger back in her mouth when the bleeding would resume. It was a tedious process but when she got to the center of the cell her diligence paid off. Hanging down was a ceramic fixture. With both hands she followed it down, eager with anticipation. To her relief, the smoothness of porcelain became the thin shell of a glass incandescent light bulb.

Zoë dropped down to her flat feet with renewed enthusiasm. Now all she had to do was find the switch, if there was one installed on the inside. She groped some of the objects that were in her way, feeling a tall file cabinet then stumbling over a piece of waist-high furniture. She felt down in its direction. It was wooden but was trimmed in a soft velvet-like material.

Back to the wall, she thought, moving back to the file cabinet caressing each of the five drawer handles. On top she felt what appeared to be cardboard boxes, one of which had something soft attached to the top of it. It felt like satin. The experience reminded her of a game she used to play with her mother. The two would sit in the dark and give each other items to feel. They each had ten seconds to guess the object's identity. It was her favorite game as a little girl. She smiled in the darkness as she remembered a game where her mother had put a cardboard box with something soft on top. It was close to her birthday and as her mom slid the box across their kitchen table, she immediately identified its identity and unwrapped the present.

In her haste Zoë reached back to the top of the file cabinet. As she grabbed for the box, she could feel the wrapping paper come loose as she clasped it between her fingers. "What the hell?" she said aloud.

In the dark her grip was clumsy and she dropped the box. It struck the wall before hitting the oak-grated floor at her feet. With a burst of light the black room turned into an intolerable brightness. The light fixture above exploded with illumination as her pupils fought to close fast enough. The sudden contrast was almost painful as she turned to shield her eyes with her empty hands.

Gradually her eyes readjusted. Slowly the interior of the freezer came into focus as heat started to resonate from the humming bulb. As Zoë looked, around her confusion turned to shock.

Chapter 29

7:19 PM
28 hours, 41 minutes left

Roman tried to balance a ten-pound bag of cat litter, another bag of vegetarian dry cat food, Trooper the kitten, and his keys as he unlocked the only entry to his apartment. Once the deadbolt was unbarred, he pushed the door open with his foot and the cat let out a resounding meow.

It was uncomfortable for him. Roman was not used to the attention he had received for the day. It had started at the restaurant where everyone from Gigi to Devon treated him with kid gloves. Then there was his visit to the 1st Precinct, and more recently, his Park Avenue doorman and a lobby full of people watched as he fumbled trying to carry the small objecting kitten and its supplies.

"Mister Sabarese, do you need a hand sir?" the pudgy doorman had asked.

"No, I've got it," he had replied as the kitten meowed.

Now at home, Trooper was scooting across the clean tile floor as Roman headed for the apartment's guest bathroom. As he switched on the florescent lights, the room glowed bright as the light reflected from the white tile wall and floor. It was going to be the first time the bathroom had been used since the space had been remodeled two years before. As he looked around, it occurred to him that he didn't have anything to deposit the bag of clay cat litter into. Then, as though it was second nature, he ripped open the bag and poured its contents around the base of the bathroom's oversized shower stall.

After getting Trooper acquainted with his facilities, Roman poured some milk into a bowl and fixed another with some food. Trooper sniffed the vegetarian mix and started eating as though he had been neglected at some shelter. Roman watched as the kitten avoided the milk.

"Water?" he asked, looking down.

A few seconds later Roman had washed the milk out of the bowl and filled it with chilled tap water. While sipping a bottle of Evian mineral water of his own, he carried the bowl with tap water back into the bathroom and put it next to the food. Again, Trooper looked at the bowl, sniffed the water, and rejected it immediately.

"What?" Roman said, looking back down at his guest before kneeling down to pet him. Trooper stopped eating and climbed up Roman's arm, licking the mouth of the bottled water.

"You've got to be kidding me," Roman said as he emptied the tap water into the toilet and refilled the bowl with the contents of his bottle of mineral water.

With Trooper content, Roman tried to get back into his routine, kicking off his shoes and flipping the TV on to catch the last bit of the news. Channel Four's local coverage filled the screen.

"NYPD have identified the body found earlier today as Noonie Jackson of Harlem, according to detectives from the 1st Precinct. Jackson was the apparent victim of a domestic dispute turned deadly as her estranged boyfriend, one Tyrone Sims, has been arrested and is in police custody at this hour charged with capital murder," the news anchor said as Roman switched the set off.

Again, he pulled his cell phone from his trousers and dialed Zoë's number.

"It's me...can't talk right now. Please leave me a message and I'll get back to you as soon as I can. Ciao."

Roman thought for a minute as he looked at the dormant cell phone. Her messages were going straight to voicemail. She was not screening her calls so the phone was either off or disabled in some way.

His mind played out a hundred scenarios ranging from a violent kidnapping to an accidental death, or *could it be,* he thought, *suicide?* As quickly as the idea entered his head it exited without a second thought. *She wasn't the type*, he reassured himself. But what *had* happened? And what will happen tomorrow when she doesn't show up for the scheduled live show for NBC?

He sat back into his deep leather couch as Trooper came into the expanse of the living room. With a leap, the kitten found its way into Roman's lap and, as it licked its paws clean, Trooper started to purr with a state of contentment.

Chapter 30

7:54 PM
28 hours, 6 minutes left

Zoë stood in shock and confusion. She had gone looking for more information about Roman and that search landed her here, an abandoned freezer locked away in the depths of the city, deep beneath the busy streets that were flooded with an abundance of people. *Ironic*, she thought. So many people, so close, and yet she was so alone.

With the light on she could take a brief inventory of everything that was held captive with her. Her expedition to find answers was now creating a new myriad of questions. The most perplexing was that in the back corner of the space was everything one would need to make an infant's nursery. It was beautiful. The furniture included a crib, changing table and matching dresser and was built and trimmed in matching cherry wood with an antique styling. Despite the thick layer of dust, she could see that someone took his or her time picking this set out. Everything had matching engravings of angels with long trumpets and the name *Evangeline* centered at the top of each piece. As she ran her hand across the smooth surface she could see that this was nothing any department store would carry. The work was custom and it was obvious that the engravings were made by hand. The crib was the piece of furniture she had bumped into when it was dark. It was dressed with a matching blanket and tiny pillows, all of which were covered in dust.

This was not what she expected and she was feeling like a voyeur that had been granted a permit into a chapter of someone's life, a hidden diary of history where she knew she didn't belong. She had found herself captive though, by the design of the freezer and what was to follow seemed inevitable. A rigged latch that couldn't be opened from the inside combined with a heavy door that had closed behind her thirty-six hours before made for an unplanned incarceration and she didn't have a choice but to make the best of her time.

Why didn't I just ignore Devon's comment, she thought. "The dungeon" he had called it a few weeks before, "where everybody hides their secrets." At first his child-like words went unnoticed, but then, as time played its unforgiving game, she began to think. The thoughts burned into her mind, especially during the last two days when she wasn't distracted on the set of *The Prosecutor.*

It's not like she wasn't at a crossroads before all this had started. Her work at Evangeline's began right after she enrolled in NYU's film school. She was well received by everyone in the restaurant, especially Devon who greeted her with a hug at the beginning of every shift. Zoë's personality made it hard for anyone not to like her. She cared about people and loved them in a natural and genuine way, the same way Melanie had loved her. The only person she had a problem with in the beginning was Roman who went out of his way to ignore her. She would make sure that he and all those who would join him at table 21 were well taken care of. This irritated him though and she eventually ended up focusing on her regular duties, which included being the hostess, answering the phones and taking to-go orders. Then one day Roman snapped at her and she began to cry. He took her aside and before the interaction was over they had sealed his apology with a hug. While always platonic, their relationship grew and before long Zoë was working with Nello, assuming some of the managerial duties. In between her classes she was seen arranging the restaurant's scheduling, inventory controls, liquor reports and other mundane clerical tasks. Roman began to depend on her for his ordering and the two bonded even more. As time passed Zoë let her guard down. She trusted and was trusted, and by people who were not in the trust business. She began to see things; meetings that seemed out of place, comments that were made about the restaurant's history, and one thing that seemed very peculiar to her. Every restaurant or bar in the city was open to the cops. They were in and out, uniformed or not, and they were welcome. Most ate for free as a sort of graft for their presence that made everyone feel safer. This was a common sight, except for Evangeline's. Cops would walk across the street to avoid being seen in front of the place. It was as though the restaurant and everyone inside didn't exist.

People talked. If she had believed any one of the rumors she would have left long before. When Melanie found out about the job, she exploded and demanded that Zoë quit. This was out of the question for her though. It was her first real form of employment and her first real money. Between tuition and the other related expenses, things were tight and Melanie was footing the entire bill. This was a way for Zoë to contribute and have some fun on her own without having to beg for extra cash all the time. Her mother agreed, under protest, and Zoë continued to work at the restaurant. As the years continued she became convinced that there wasn't a shred of proof that anyone at Evangeline's was in any way connected to the mafia or to organized crime of any fashion. It wasn't until her newly acquired fame, which brought the prying eyes of the media, that the subject was even broached again. It wasn't until a copy of *The Observer* found its way in front of her that she knew she had to dig deeper. It was one thing to hear a rumor; it was quite another to see it in black and white complete with full color pictures, even if it was *The Observer.*

Perched on top of the nursery furniture were stacks of wrapped presents. Most had tags that were addressed to Eve, Bettina or both and a large teddy bear covered in dust was perched atop the changing table that was next to a five-drawer file cabinet. Most of the stuff was damp and moldy. Upon closer examination she could see a water line that made a consistent mark a foot above the oak-grated floor that encompassed the interior of the freezer. *This place was prone to flood*, she surmised.

As her curiosity worked at her, Zoë tried to open the bottom two file drawers but both were rusted shut. She kicked the cabinet out of frustration as the third drawer rolled out six inches before stopping in its metal tracks. She grabbed the handle and opened it the rest of the way. Packed into the three-foot-deep drawer were hundreds of manila file folders. All were neatly organized with dark green hangers and neatly typed index tabs. The first one read *Dubai.*

She carefully pulled the hanger out of its place and thumbed through the dozen or so files it held. Most contained redundant balance sheets, different variations of the same business plan, and detailed profit projections. To her, the numbers were staggering. Despite the fact that her own net worth had already exceeded a million dollars, she had never actually seen the money since it had been invested by Melanie where it was safe and secure in places she was not aware. The numbers listed on the files eclipsed her own though, and the profit projections were even more staggering.

The initial investment was sixteen million U.S. dollars with three principal investors that were represented by a series of initials.

RTS had invested almost thirteen and a half million, *NF* was in at one point eight million and *G* was vested at eight hundred thousand. It was easy to conclude that *RTS* stood for Roman Sabarese. His middle name *was* Theodore, after all. *NF,* it was safe to guess, represented Nello Falcone, although it was a mystery as to how a restaurant manager would have almost two million dollars to invest in anything. The third initial, *G*, was the real mystery. Roman's dad was Ray Sabarese and his mother was Lucia. Roman had one brother, Ray Junior, who had died seven years before. *Was this person a Sabarese,* she pondered *or one of Roman's darker associates?*

The next ten files contained detailed construction reports and handwritten notes from an independent American engineer who had surveyed every facet of the elaborate construction process. Tucked into the notes was a large blueprint of the entire project. *This was huge*, she thought to herself. Eight four-crane gantries on four separate canals spanning over two hundred acres of prime Dubai waterfront property.

While the size and complexity of the project were more than she could comprehend, the profit projections were even more unbelievable. A six-page report had been prepared by an uptown accountant and was signed off by Max Weintraub. With the sixteen million dollar investment in place, the three principal investors stood to reap over two hundred and ten million in net, after tax, profits over a fifteen year period with the lion's share going to the largest investor, *RTS* - Roman.

It was impressive and gave her an inside view of a man she only knew half of, the part he wanted her to know. This was, after all, why she was here investigating, broaching her veil of accessibility, to find out who he really was. Dubai, while a pleasant surprise, wasn't what she was looking for. This project was, by all appearances, legitimate. What she wanted to see – what she *had* to see - was proof of something more sinister, something that could reveal Roman's reputed past. The obvious was irrefutable. His father was the indicted don of the New York mafia, *but where did that leave his son?* The questions began to give her a headache.

A month before Zoë had watched the TV news reports shot from the numerous helicopters that were hovering over the Sabarese's Staten Island estate on that fateful Thanksgiving Day. Black-clad federal agents had escorted Ray Senior out of the mansion while scores more roved every inch of the property looking for clues. It occupied the local news cycle for weeks, but despite the high profile nature of the case, Roman, Ray's only living son, was never mentioned, not until Tuesday morning's *Observer* article and that was her fault. This attention had everything to do with her and while Roman may have been the catalyst for some of the juiciest city gossip in years, alone, he wouldn't have raised such an exposé.

The last file in the Dubai hanger was labeled *Payments*. The initials *RTS* marked the first page where sums totaling thirteen point four million had been detailed in a series of line items that corresponded with overseas wire codes. Each one was dated, showing the departure date from a bank in the Cayman Islands and the receipt date at another bank in Dubai. The next page was labeled with *NF* and detailed one large wire transfer in the amount of one point eight million from a retirement investment account in the name of Nello and Marjory Falcone, which confirmed her assumption about *those* initials. The third was labeled with a large *G* and had attached to it a photocopy of a check from the Zoë Green investment account for eight hundred thousand dollars. It was dated September 1st, 1999, and was signed by her mother, Melanie Greene.

Zoë didn't know what to think. *Why wasn't I told about this?* she thought to herself. What had been a mission of disclosure was now becoming increasingly complicated as she placed all the papers back in their respective places and the hanger back into the drawer.

She went through every file and what she found made her so tired that she felt her eyes go heavy. She thumbed through every tax return, real estate contract and restaurant vendor agreement. It all fit the scenario that Roman, besides being the son of Ray Senior, was legitimate.

Chapter 31

8:10 PM
27 hours, 50 minutes left

Fitz sipped on his orange flavored Gatorade as he returned to his desk on the top floor of the 1st Precinct. Like a woman with morning sickness, he was used to the regular trips to the station's men's room that was down the hall from his office. The part he wasn't used to was the constant stares he would receive on his many returns. Pity was not an ingredient Captain Stanley Fitzgerald, Chief of Detectives, swallowed easily.

"You've got visitors in your office boss," a subordinate said as Fitz took another swig of the ice-cold orange liquid.

"Thanks Hector."

"IA," he whispered.

"Lucky me."

Fitz opened the door to see two men in suits seated in front of his desk. They more resembled a pair of FBI agents than NYPD detectives.

"Captain," Detective Sergeant Robert McNamara said, holding out an extended hand.

Unlike television, the internal affairs unit of the NYPD had a good working relationship with the middle management of the local precincts. They had to. Most of the cops that were under investigation were either new recruits or had been on the job less than three years. Most of the cases investigated by internal affairs were related to public interaction and that occurred on the street level with the uniformed officers on patrol. Without a seasoned commanding officer to stand behind these investigations the entire process would be undermined. It was about the discipline and control of the officers who carried the liability of the City of New York with them on a daily basis.

"Hey Bob," Fitz said as he gripped the man's hand with a solid shake.

"This is Detective Sergeant Paul Wajowoski. He's just joined our unit down here."

"Paul, nice to meet you," Fitz said with a nod.

"Before we start, I need to ask, how are you holding up? I heard about the cancer. Tough break man."

"One day at a time Bob. Thanks for asking."

"Look, you probably know why we're here. It's just part of the routine. Word is you had a visit from one of the city's old friends. One Roman Sabarese."

"I did," Fitz replied.

"Anything you want to tell us?"

"Well, not really…" Fitz said, smiling.

"I know it's a stretch, but is Mr. Sabarese registered in your cache of confidential informants?"

"Nope, but you knew that already."

"Had to ask, you know the drill…"

"So what gives?"

"Roman came to me looking for help," Fitz explained.

"Really?" the investigator said with a chuckle.

"Really."

"Look, I don't have to tell you what we're up against here. The head of organized crime waltzes in to your office in broad daylight and people are going to talk. It's a fact of life."

"It's probably the meetings in the back alley they should be worried about," Fitz added.

"You meet him in the back alley?" Detective Wajowoski asked as he thumbed through some of the files in the veteran captain's desk.

"Bob, I'm powerless here. The man's a citizen. His family pays over two million a year in city taxes alone. You want me to tell him he's not allowed in his own police precinct? That he can't talk to me, his public servant?"

"I think something stinks here," Wajowoski said.

"Oh, I get it…you're the bad cop," Fitz said as Bob smiled.

"What Detective Wajowoski is trying to say is…"

"I get it. Really, I do. I wasn't born yesterday and I know it looks bad but you have to remember that you trust me with the foundational workings of this precinct, a six million dollar capital budget and two point three million in annual payroll. I make a thousand complex decisions a week, half of which have serious consequences for those involved. Either you trust me or you don't," Fitz said, spent of any remaining patience.

It was a half hour after the detectives from IA had left the 1st Precinct and Detective Captain Stanley Fitzgerald could feel the tension boil in his stomach. Most people had their ways of dealing with conflict and anger; some didn't, and those people were usually a danger to others or themselves. Many of the regular remedies involved a punching bag, screaming in the shower or driving aggressively in rush hour traffic. For Fitz, his solution sat in the basement of his own precinct house.

All cops had to re-qualify with their service weapons. In the late seventies, because of the high cost of sending officers out of the city for firearms training, a firing range was constructed below street level. At times, those on the sidewalk could hear the barrage of gunfire that emanated from deep within the building's foundation.

Fitz made his way to the basement where he found a line twenty officers long, all of whom where waiting for the same thing.

"Go ahead Captain," one of the waiting offered.

"Are you sure?" Fitz asked humbly.

"There's plenty we can all learn by watching you shoot sir," he said as the line moved aside to let Fitz pass onto the stalls of the range. As he took his position donning a pair of earmuffs and a set of clear protective glasses, the other officers in the shooting stalls around him stopped and watched.

Breathe, stance, aim and squeeze, he thought to himself as he had done a thousand times before. In twenty-nine years as a cop with the NYPD he had never shot another. But that didn't mean he wasn't prepared.

Breathe, stance, aim and squeeze.

Pop Pop……. Pop Pop…….. Pop Pop……. Pop Pop…….. Pop Pop…….. Pop Pop.

As Fitz hit a switch on the side of the stall, a paper target started to float back in his direction. The other officers in the neighboring stalls took off their clear glasses and the waiting men in the line behind moved closer to gain a better view as the paper, a cutout silhouette of a man, came up to the firing line. Six double-tap rounds had been fired in under three seconds and Fitz, at the age of forty-eight and suffering from renal cancer and pumped up with chemo, pain killers and a gallon of Gatorade, put all twelve shots into two holes, both of which weren't any larger than a silver dollar, one at the heart and the other dead square on the silhouetted man's forehead. One of the officers in line started to clap and then the rest followed with a hearty applause that was usually reserved for bachelor parties or the opening monologue for *The Tonight Show*. For some shooters, the target represented a person, a mean older brother, an ex-wife, a perp. But in Fitz's case, today the cutout was Detective Paul Wajowoski from NYPD Internal Affairs.

Chapter 32

8:40 PM
27 hours, 20 minutes left

If there was a silver lining to being held captive it was that Zoë was forced to sit and ponder her life and realize that despite this captivity, she hadn't missed the things that many use to measure both their success and hers. In recent years she had been blessed with all the material things that so many sacrificed their lives for. Many of the people she had been acquainted with over the years needed those things to feel a sense of completeness. The cars, trips, jewelry and the oversized home had been a tangible benefit of her success but not something she couldn't live without.

Zoë and her mother had an annual tradition that had started when she was just four years old. It was something that was always strange to her, considering that Melanie was Jewish, and yet she insisted on raising her only daughter as a Catholic. In keeping with this, every year a month before Christmas, a friend would drive them to a spruce tree farm in White Plains. The two would stomp through the snow and examine seemingly every tree on the small five-acre farm. After two or more hours of detailed examination she would pick the greenest and fullest one she could find. After lugging the tree back to their brownstone in the Village that first year, they erected it in the living room. Melanie then pulled out several new boxes of decorations that she had been hiding in the hall closet.

"What are we doing?" Zoë asked.

"Decorating our beautiful tree," her mother answered.

"But then we won't be able to see its true beauty and what a good job I did picking it out," her four year old mind had deducted. After that, the tradition continued. The only difference as of late, was that Zoë would rent a car and the two of them would head north and make a formal weekend of it, spending the night in a quaint bed and breakfast before heading back to the city.

I am that bare Christmas tree, she thought to herself, *and all the tinsel and store-bought decorations were going to do was hide my true identity.* Her core was solid and from it branched an abundance of talents that didn't need to be accessorized or modified. It was these talents and these alone that would take her far beyond her present place in life to new heights that she had only dreamed about. Now all she had to do was figure out how to get out of the freezer.

Upstairs, Devon stood at the door to the women's restroom of Evangeline's for what seemed like twenty minutes. While some were afraid of heights, confining spaces, spiders or snakes, Devon's greatest fear was going into the wrong bathroom. Roman had, after seeing an article about the projected high tide and strange weather patterns that would plague Manhattan over the weekend, ordered the dishwasher to go to the sub-basement and check on the sump-pump. Since the area was prone to collect rainwater and flood occasionally, a commercial grade pump was installed and attached to a float switch, the type commonly seen in the bilge of a boat; the type that's activated by rising water. The problem had always been that the large pump drew an even larger portion of electricity, thereby tripping its corresponding fuse in the circuit box located on a higher level.

"Hello. It's Devon. I...I need to come in," he announced, stammering his words as he took a deep breath, closed his eyes and entered the restroom. "Hello. It's Devon. Don't be scared," he continued. "It's just me."

Refusing to open his eyes, he felt for the access door's handle. In his hand were Roman's personal set of keys. Normally Devon would just retrieve the door's key from a small nail that was around the restaurant's office. When he went to get it though, it was gone.

"What do you mean the key's not there?" Roman had protested as he handed over his own set of master keys.

Devon's next feat was to find the key without opening his eyes. The idea of being able to see the inside of the women's bathroom excited him, and in turn, made him feel guilty. *Zoë used this bathroom*, he told himself, *and this was her private place.*

To his surprise though, the door was already unlocked. Now a new fear took over. The long stone stairway in front of him looked like something out of one of the fifties era horror films he enjoyed watching. Films like *Frankenstein* and *The Wolf Man* had cavernous passages just like this one. An order was an order though, and again, he took a deep breath and proceeded down the long flight of steps.

Inside the freezer Zoë continued to look through the file cabinet. In contrast to the last, the second drawer held what appeared to be a series of personal things including a heart-shaped box of candy, a stuffed white rabbit and envelopes filled with letters and greeting cards. Zoë's first instinct was to close it back. This was voyeuristic and not her nature, but then she noticed something that made her open the drawer completely. It was a faded newspaper clipping with a black and gray picture of a woman in a nurse's uniform complete with a traditional starched nurse's cap. The article had appeared on the thirty-second page and was cropped next to an ad for women's underwear at Macy's. Below the picture was a caption that was both simple and to the point.

Negro Nursing Student Murdered In Back Alley

The body of twenty-eight year old Bettina Cooper was discovered in a back alley at the intersection of 9th Street and 4th Avenue in Brooklyn early yesterday morning by detectives from the 78th Precinct.

Attached to the article about the nursing student was another clipping, only this one was from the front page of *The New York Times.*

Veteran Detective, a Local Hero, Slain

The entire front page was filled with testimonials, an op-ed from the mayor and more pictures of the slain detective who was identified as William Stewart. *Why would Roman keep all of this?* she asked herself. And then she saw what appeared to be a handwritten letter to the dead nursing student.

Bettina,

Every day is heavier than the next without you by my side. I awake not knowing I'm going to make it through the day and yet, somehow it happens. My last words to you were, "they will have to accept you." Those words haunt me every waking minute. I don't know how to cope with these feelings without you. I would pledge the rest of my life to take back that day if I could, to reconstruct it and make the subtle changes that would have made all the difference.

I miss you and your daughter more than you can know. You live in my thoughts and dreams.

Eternally yours,
Roman

This last item revealed more than all the other things combined. While they had grown close, Roman had never talked about his past or the events that made up this tragic day in 1974. She had always wondered why he hadn't married. The man, she assumed, wasn't gay, not that it would have been a problem if he had been. She worked in the entertainment industry. Those of alternative lifestyles and faiths for that matter, were *as common as they should be in the rest of society,* she thought to herself. Those who had little or no tolerance for people that were different than them didn't last very long in her business. It was a self-filtering occupational hazard and one she was more than happy to embrace. Still, *Roman, gay? No way,* she concluded. He was visibly interested in the attractive women that came into the restaurant. Interest however, was the limit of his emotional involvement. Even when she had prompted him, even after securing a phone number from an exceptionally attractive woman that had spied him while seated on a stool at his own bar, Roman simply smiled and ignored the suggestion. *This went deeper,* she was beginning to understand. Now she could see his injured heart. Evangeline's was, besides being one of the city's finest and most sought-out Italian restaurants, a mecca for young lovers who either shared a first date, celebrated an anniversary or proposed a marriage that would hopefully lead to many celebrated anniversaries. Now she could appreciate the irony. It was a paradox that a man who lost so much in the way of love, was himself, the owner of an establishment that was a beacon for lovers. *The daily reminders must have been heart-wrenching,* she thought. It had also been strange to her that a man who appeared fearless was so phobic of something most took for granted, some more than others. It was for the first time that she saw the parallel in her own life and that of her mother. Zoë had also been a casualty of lost love albeit not directly. Melanie, her mother, had lost her true love in a different war and in a different place. She had grown up under the guise of a single mother who displayed the rigors of a self-reliant existence without needing the support of anyone. Growing up as the daughter of Melanie Greene she had learned a long time ago, had certainly left its mark, a mark she was more than happy to embrace. It was this spirit of independence and self-reliance that had been passed down, day after day, that reinforced her own sense of self-worth and determination.

Feeling overwhelmed by what she was seeing, Zoë sat against the edge of the cherry wood crib. As she looked back over at the open drawer, a corner of a partially concealed black and white photograph caught her eye. Carefully, she pried it loose as the old glossy surface tried to stick to the paper it was lodged against. The picture was of a small brigade of uniformed infantrymen that were standing in front of an Army helicopter. At the bottom written with a pen was a caption: *Sergeant Roman Sabarese, Corporal Horace Greene, "Bubba" Futch and the PA boys.*

Horace Green? My father Horace? she thought, almost alarmed. *In the same picture as Roman? Why hadn't he ever told me?* She was immediately disappointed. He could have given her so much information about him; a man that had created her and in doing so, passed along so many traits. Her own mother was vague at best and when she did talk about him she could never do so without crying. Needless to say, it was a topic that very rarely came up in their home. *Roman could have told me. I have so many questions,* she thought as her mood turned negative and her head started to throb again. Then she heard it.

Devon had made his way into the sub-basement and in classic Devon style, was making a loud and clumsy passage. Zoë stopped for a second and listened.

"Devon! Is that you? Heeelp!" she cried. "Get me out of here!"

The dishwasher bent down to look at the sump pump. It was intact and the reset button that was on the unit itself was pushed in. The pump was ready. And then he heard her muffled voice. "Devon…is that you?"

Oh my God! he thought to himself. *It's a ghost!*

"It's Zoë's ghost! She lives in the dungeon!" he yelled out loud as he ran up the stairs and into the women's restroom. Unfortunately, an unsuspecting patron was entering at the same time and came face to face with a flustered Devon. To him, being in the women's restroom, the holy shrine for all things female, was bad enough. To be in there when a woman was also there was unthinkable. In a panic he screamed and in doing so lost the contents of his bladder. Mortified past a simple state of embarrassment, Devon bolted up the remaining stairs and made his way back into the kitchen where he went back to work at his sink, not before splashing some dishwater on his lap to cover his untimely accident.

Chapter 33

8:44 PM
27 hours, 16 minutes left

While he loved his job, Fitz had grown to hate his position. He joined the NYPD in 1970, full of idealism and vigor. This was only multiplied when he was promoted to detective during the summer of 1973. *Those were the years*, he thought. His tasks in recent years had been relegated to managing other detectives, something he detested so much it had left a pit in his stomach. This case changed everything. Now he could hit the street.

He started by making some specially placed calls, dispatching two plain-clothes detectives from his sex crimes squad to rouse the usual suspects. They rattled the cages of the most notorious offenders in the area, those that were left at least.

A cursory check of Zoë's credit card produced two charges since Monday. The first was to a rental car company. According to the clerk, she had rented a metallic blue 2000 Millennium Edition Corvette for the week with a voucher. The credit card was required as a security deposit and the car wasn't due back until January 2nd, 2000. The second charge was for a newspaper and another Diet

Coke purchased at a street newsvendor just a block from Evangeline's. Fitz picked up the phone.

"Dispatch, I need a citywide BOLO for a blue metallic 2000 Corvette, Jersey plates, AVC-658."

Ten minutes later Fitz was on the street. It felt good to get out of the office and he enjoyed the fresh air. As he passed Washington Market Park he loosened his jacket. The cold wasn't that bad without the wind. Wind in the city could be brutal as it whipped through the tight confines of the buildings like a funnel, channeling the frigid waves of air in one direction or another. Tonight was different. It was still and peaceful. A few older kids sat in the park, talking and listening to music. Around them were a half dozen orange embers that appeared in the dark. *Cigarettes. If they could spend a week in my shoes,* he thought to himself, *or an hour in the oncology unit with a steady channel of chemo flowing into an open vein.*

Fitz knew that he would, at one point or another, have to call Roman. To make things easier on himself and his career, he darted inside a corner Rite Aid drug store and purchased a disposable cell phone with its own number and a prepaid calling plan with a thousand minutes. He paid with cash and gave an anonymous name. Five minutes later he was back on the street as he continued to walk on the west side and pass the front entrance to Evangeline's, stopping to get his bearings. To the north was Duane Street and around the corner, his destination, Street Sense, Inc., DBA, City News.

And that's when he saw it. Parked on the northeast corner of the park grounds was a metallic blue 2000 Corvette. Fitz made a brisk walk towards the car. *Sure enough,* he thought, *Jersey plate on the rear, AVC-658.*

"Car 112 to dispatch," Fitz said into his Motorola portable radio.

"Car 112, go ahead Captain."

"Car 112 has BOLO contact at the corner of Greenwich and Duane. Cancel the BOLO and send me a crime scene unit please and a city hook when you get a chance."

"Ten-four car 112, CSU and tow truck en route."

It was ironic that Fitz's radio tag was car 112. He hadn't been in an actual squad car in years. The radio handle denoted NYPD command, a throwback from the earlier days when all the top brass had cars and everyone else pounded the pavement on foot patrol.

As he approached the car it was apparent it had been there for a while. Five parking tickets were clipped beneath the driver's side wiper and an iron tire boot had been affixed on the rear passenger side. A lime green decal had been stuck on the back window indicating that it was time to tow the car to impound for the lengthy parking violation. Fitz continued to look around the car for anything that might stick out. The meter time had been long expired with its digital display blinking a red signal. Five feet from the curb was a six-foot-high black wrought iron fence that segregated the park from the sidewalk. As he looked around the meter, something shiny caught his attention. Fitz felt a soft sliver of pain as he bent over to examine it closer. A new lipstick container sat next to the meter's base. As he stood, a blue and white NYPD tow truck from parking enforcement pulled up to a stop with it's brakes squeaking from neglect.

"Hey Captain, I was just about to get that one but I thought I would take my break first," he said, yelling from the truck's open window.

"Did you happen to notice there was a BOLO out on this car?"

"No sir, I missed that."

"Pay closer attention next time. A CSU will be here in a minute to process the scene. When they're finished, take it to case active holding."

Case active holding was the area of the city's impound garage that was segregated from all the rest. Vehicles that were material evidence in an active case were kept there, fenced off from the rest as an act of preservation.

Fitz looked inside the car. Nothing was out of place. There were no obvious signs of a struggle and the interior was as clean as when she picked it up at the rental company. Then he pulled out the newly purchased cell phone and called Roman.

"Hey, it's Fitz," take down this number, 212-431-1112. It will be our only way of contact for a while."

"Got it," Roman confirmed.

"I found the car."

"What car?"

"Zoë rented a car for the week."

"Oh that, now I remember. She had a voucher from some film festival, Sundance or something like that. You know, celebrity stuff. It expired at the end of this year and she thought it would be fun. She didn't want to depend on the taxis, what with all the extra people in town for the new year."

"Well, I'm standing next to it."

"Where?"

"Right across the street from your restaurant."

"I'm coming over."

"No Roman, please don't do that. Let me handle this. There's nothing to see. It's clean."

"As you wish."

"You answered my question anyway. Can we meet at Melanie Greene's in a few hours?"

"Sure, I'll head that way as soon as I'm done here. Thanks Fitz."

"In the meantime, I'll let you know if I find anything out," Fitz said as the detective's new cell phone beeped with a disconnecting tone.

As soon as he put the phone back into his pocket, another blue and white truck pulled up to the Corvette. This time it was a CSU van. As it parked, Fitz waved the technicians over to the lipstick container.

"Bag this please," he ordered.

"Got it," the first one said, picking it up with a set of tweezers and depositing it into a marked Ziploc bag.

"I need a full work-up on this one. Dust it inside and out. And I need it ASAP."

"What's the case number?"

"We don't have it yet. Just put my name on all the paperwork. Anybody gives you grief, have 'em call me."

"Will do Captain."

Within seconds, one of the CSU techs had an unlocking device, a thin blade of stainless steel called a slim-jim out and he was sliding it in between the car's driver side window and the exterior fiberglass skin of the door. Three seconds later the plastic lock on the inside popped up and the tech's gloved hand opened the door.

"Don't you think you should have dusted that door handle?" Fitz asked.

"Sorry Captain but this car's been here a while. That door handle's got the prints of every homeless guy in a four block radius."

It was their thing, Fitz thought, acknowledging that they were right.

"Just go the extra mile on this one, okay?"

"You're the boss," the tech replied.

Once the tow truck came back to pick up the rental Corvette, Fitz made his way to Duane Street. A small newsstand sat on the sidewalk and sold everything from candy bars, to *Playboy* magazines, to souvenir tee shirts to fresh copies of *The Observer.*

"Are you Phil McGee, Street Sense, Inc. and/or City News?" Fitz asked the man, opening his overcoat to expose his gold shield and gun, "NYPD."

"I'm the owner," the gruff man said.

"Were you working this last Monday night?"

"It's just me and I've been staying until midnight all week…you know, with all the tourists in town."

"Do you remember a transaction at about 11:45, a young biracial woman? I think she bought a newspaper and a Diet Coke."

"Zoë? Sure, but she didn't get no paper. She bought an *Observer*. I rememba' cuz she and Mr. Roman were on the cover. Some kinda nerve these rags got printin' that shit."

"Yeah, hey, did you notice anything strange about her, or anyone she might have been with?"

"No. Me and the wife love her show. She's a pistol that one."

"So, she was alone?" Fitz asked, trying to confirm what he already knew.

"Yep, all by herself."

"Do you remember where she went after she made her purchase?"

"Hey, Detective, is everything alright, I mean, is Zoë Okay? I'd hate to think..."

"She's fine. Someone tried to mug her and she fought him off."

"That's Zoë. Like I said, she's a pistol," he said smiling at the thought. "Let me think. You know, I'm pretty sure she walked back to Greenwich."

"Did you see which way she turned?"

"Nope. Sorry. Another customer came right after her. I do remember that she was pretty upset about the story in *The Observer.*"

"Understandable," Fitz agreed. "Your next customer, a regular? Did it seem like he was following Zoë?"

"Now that you mention it, he could have been. He had an expensive camera around his neck and one of those photographer vests. You know, the kind with all those pockets."

"A safari vest?"

"Yeah, one of those. Hey, we'd hate to see something happen to Zoë. I mean, she's just starting to go after that lady for getting her kids killed and all."

"What?" Fitz replied, confused by his statement.

"The show, she's a real pistol that one."

* * *

An hour later, Fitz parked a city issued charcoal Crown Victoria in front of the Greene family's brownstone, ignoring the expired meter that rose up from the sidewalk. Roman opened Melanie's front door as the detective crested the top step.

"Come on in," Roman offered. "Anything to drink?"

"No thanks, I'm fine."

"Zoë's room is upstairs."

"Hi Detective," Melanie said, joining the two from the kitchen.

"Mrs. Greene. Where do you keep your coats?" Fitz asked.

"Down here on the main floor," Melanie answered as she opened their coat closet. "The only coat missing is her leather one from Cannes. Everything else has been accounted for."

"I see that you are taking down your tree," Fitz remarked, pointing over at the bare Christmas tree erected in the corner of the living room.

"That's one of our traditions. It never gets decorated," Melanie explained.

"Let's see Zoë's room."

"It's on the top floor. Sorry, no elevator."

The three climbed the wood trimmed steps to the fourth floor. Once at the top, Fitz could feel a wave of vertigo, a common side effect of the chemotherapy.

"You okay?" Roman asked as he put a hand on his shoulder and Fitz grabbed the railing.

"Yeah, thanks," Fitz said.

"Zoë's room is to the right," Melanie instructed, pointing down the long hall. A few seconds later Fitz was pushing the six-panel antique door open with the tips of his fingers as the hinges creaked with age.

"She says that door has character. She wouldn't let me replace it," Melanie explained nervously as Fitz just looked around.

"I see signs of a pet."

"Trooper. She rescued him from the highway upstate a month or so ago."

"Where is the animal now?" Fitz asked.

"Oh, with Roman."

"Really?" Fitz replied with a smile that crossed his face as Roman nodded back, shaking his head.

"Vegetarian cat food and Evian bottled water. Trooper's got it rough," Roman added.

"I'm sorry," Fitz said with a chuckle.

"We're getting along just fine," Roman replied, looking in Melanie's direction.

"Sorry. I know he's high maintenance," she added.

"How have you and Zoë been getting along?" Fitz asked of Melanie.

"Fine. She wasn't crazy about this NBC show tomorrow…she hates live shoots but we worked through it, like we always do."

"Do you think, and I'm just suggesting, the pressure might be getting to her?"

"She's been doing well. I mean, of course she's had bad days, we all do, but Zoë's tough, you know?"

"I do. You've done a fine job Mrs. Green."

"When I talked to her on Monday she was all about getting some calamari. That's seemed to be all she had on her mind," Roman added.

"Roman, do you think she would have told you if she was having any problems coping?" Fitz asked.

"We talked about everything. I guess that makes me her sounding board, or one of them," Roman said, acknowledging Melanie. "So, yes, I guess it does. If there was something she had to get off her chest I would have probably heard about it."

"Mrs. Green, any strange phone calls?"

"No, not since that Schultze guy."

"Andrew Schultze, right?"

"Yes. He called twice actually. The first time he sounded sweet. When I asked that he not call again, he phoned right back and said the most vile things…mostly anti-Semitic and racial jargon. And then the next morning he left this," Melanie explained as she pulled a small rope noose out of a paper bag she had been holding. Fitz took the noose and looked it over.

"I made some calls. Andrew Schultze was in New Jersey early Tuesday morning," Fitz announced.

"Did they arrest him?" Melanie asked.

"No ma'am. He was found in the middle of the highway, dead...killed actually. The matter is still under investigation."

"Oh..." she replied as the two looked over at Roman with a silent pause.

*　　　*　　　*

Fitz pushed open the front door of Evangeline's as everyone who sat at the bar looked in his direction.

"Captain," Nello called out as he reached across the bar with an extended hand.

"You must be Nello Falcone," Fitz replied, shaking the man's hand.

"Come back into the kitchen. We can talk there," he offered as the two walked through the dining room.

Fitz looked around as though he were in a museum. He had been the first member of the NYPD to enter the establishment in twenty plus years. While the patrons didn't pay much attention, the staff watched him closely as the police detective's gun and badge reflected the candlelight that flickered from the different tables as he passed, walking towards the kitchen.

"So I guess you know why I'm here," Fitz speculated.

"Of course," Nello replied. "Can I get you some coffee?"

"No thanks, I'm fine."

"What can I do to help?" Nello offered.

"When was the last time you saw Ms. Greene?"

"On Monday. Zoë came in for dinner and stayed for an hour or so."

"Did you see her leave? Was she with anyone?"

"No, we had a vent motor over the main grill smoke up. I had to come in here and fix it."

"So you didn't see her leave?"

"I didn't. When all the commotion was over, she was gone."

"Did she come with anyone?"

"Nope," Nello answered, shaking his head. "Now that I think about it, she never brought *anyone* here. Is that strange?"

"I don't know man. Could be."

"I'm sorry I couldn't be any more help Captain."

"There is one more thing Nello. You wouldn't happen to know anything about the death of a guy named Ariel Zillo or anyone else who may have expired in the last week, or more specifically, since this last Monday?"

"Who? Never heard of him," Nello replied pointing around the kitchen. "Nope, my life is right here."

"Okay. That's all for now," Fitz said as Nello went back into the dining room to get Jess and Lisa. He continued looking around the busy kitchen as the staff of five worked feverishly turning out steamy plates of food. They seemed to ignore him as he strolled around, looking up into the large hood over the main grill. The vent motor was new and freshly installed, confirming what Nello had told him.

"Captain, this is Lisa and Jess, two of our regular waitresses," Nello said as the twins entered behind him.

"Nice to meet you both," Fitz said as they came closer, half sitting on an adjacent counter. "I just have a few questions and then I'll let you get back to work."

"Anything for Zoë," Lisa said.

"When was the last time you saw her?"

"Monday, about 11:15 PM. She ordered her calamari special."

"Special?" Fitz asked.

"Yeah. It's not on the menu. She concocted the recipe herself when she worked here a few years ago. Roman hated it so we only made the dish for her."

"I'm intrigued. What makes this calamari so different?"

"Garlic and curry. It'll make your eyes water," Jess added.

"Wow. Zoë liked spicy food?"

"Like it? She loved it. We always told her she should have worked at a Mexican place."

"Did you see her leave that night?"

"No. It was crazy until 1:00 AM. The smoke got pretty heavy in here from the exhaust fan. We thought we were going to have to evacuate the customers," Lisa explained.

"Yeah. It was crazy," Jess said.

"Any friends with her?"

"No. She never came in with anyone. Her and Roman are pretty tight…"

"Not like that crappy paper says though," Lisa insisted.

"Yeah," her sister added.

"I get it. It's cool," Fitz agreed. "Anyone want to hurt Zoë…that you know of?"

"There was this guy…Schultze something. He came in here last week."

"And that banker," Lisa added.

"Yeah…cute in a creepy momma's boy kinda way."

"When was the last time you saw him?"

"Oh it's been a year…"

"Or two maybe," Lisa tried to calculate, putting an index finger to her chin.

"Eighteen months," Jess estimated.

"I think I see. He's not in the picture."

"No. He's not coming back," Jess announced as the two giggled.

"I'm sorry? What did I miss?" Fitz asked.

"Nothing," both girls replied in unison.

"Well, I think that about covers it," Fitz announced as Roman entered the kitchen.

"Roman…" Fitz said, extending his hand.

"Thanks for coming over," Evangeline's owner said as he waved Devon over from where the dishwasher was elbow deep in a stainless steel sink cleaning a stack of dirty pots. "Fitz, this is Devon, our dishwasher and busboy. He's very fond of Zoë."

"Hi Devon," Fitz said as the large man approached.

"Hi. I'm Devon. I wash dishes."

"Just answer the questions Dev," Roman instructed.

"Yes Mister Roman," he replied with a simple tone and his head down as though he had just been chastised.

"Devon?" Fitz asked. "I understand that you and Zoë are good friends."

"I love Zoë. She's my girlfriend."

"Really," Fitz said with a smile. "I bet that makes you feel pretty good."

"Yes sir," Devon replied with a bigger grin.

"When was the last time you saw her?"

"Oh…the other day."

"Monday?"

"The other Monday…yes sir. She gave me a hug. I like hugs. I like Zoë. She's my girlfriend."

"Do you know where she is?" Fitz asked as Devon stared off into space. "Devon!" he continued, snapping his fingers.

"Ghosts…ghosts in the dungeon," he replied as Fitz looked over at Roman.

"Devon? What are you talking about?" Roman asked.

"Ghosts are in the secret dungeon. I heard them yelling. Zoë's a ghost. I think she's dead."

"Zoë's dead? How do you know this?" Fitz asked with a surprised tone.

"Ghosts are in the dungeon."

"Okay Devon. You can go back to work," Roman offered, shaking his head as the dishwasher returned to his sink.

"Let me do some more poking around. I've got to be frank with you. It doesn't look good. We've got nothing to go on."

"She's scheduled to do a live show tomorrow. If she doesn't show up then we need to escalate this," Roman decided.

"I don't know if it can wait," Fitz said as he threw down an early edition of *The Observer* newspaper. "Have you seen this yet?"

Roman picked up the paper and unfolded it to see, in bold letters, the striking headline:

Hey Mad Man: Where's Zoë?

Below the one-inch-high letters was a full color picture of himself striking at the photog that had been in the alley on Tuesday morning. Roman dropped the paper on the counter. "The guy was hiding behind my dumpster. He rushed me in the alley so I took his camera and hit him. It was an instant response. I thought the camera was destroyed."

"He's not taken any police action. The guy's probably worried that he's just as guilty. But this raises the stakes."

Roman rested his head in his hands as the cell phone in his pocket started to ring.

"Yeah."

"It's Melanie."

"Hey. Fitz is here at the restaurant. We're going over things now."

"Have you seen today's edition of *The Observer?*" her voice alerted over the phone as Fitz started to leave.

"Hold on Mel...Fitz, thanks," Roman said, nodding.

"I'll be in touch," Fitz answered as he headed for the door.

"The guy ambushed me in the back alley. He was trying to get a picture of Zoë."

"How do they know she's missing?"

"I don't know, but I intend to find out," Roman replied with determination.

"What do we do?"

"Hold tight. If she doesn't show for the live broadcast tomorrow we won't have a choice but to go public, make an appeal and expand the search."

"I hope you're right Roman."

"Me too."

Chapter 34

10:43 PM
25 hours, 17 minutes left

As he left, Fitz stood in front of Evangeline's, debating whether or not to go around back and examine the alley. He imagined a myriad of pictures being taken as he stood in front of the former mob clubhouse. *IA would have a field day if they could see this*, he thought to himself. Out of instinct he looked back over his shoulder at the building across the street...and that's when he saw it.

"I'll be damned," he said aloud.

* * *

The walls of the apartment housing the DSS detail were in disrepair. When the space was retrofitted for surveillance, a tech had taken a discount brand curtain rod and mounted it to the plaster-covered wall over the room's large bay window. With all the different agents that came and went through the flat and the constant peering and handling of the curtains, the screws that held the cover in place became loose and their foundation deteriorated. As the intern agent on duty pulled the curtain aside to look across the street it gave way.

"Grab it!" Special Agent Joel Kenyon yelled.

"Shit!" the intern blurted out, trying to hold the one side that had come loose.

"Hold it still!" Kenyon ordered.

The intern grabbed the rod and held the curtain back in place to cover the telescopes and video cameras. Kenyon jabbed a pencil into the metal rod bracket and then through the loose hole in the plaster. The two then stood back for a second and admired their impromptu handiwork. A second later, it fell again.

"Shit!" the senior agent yelled this time.

"You hold it in place. I'll run down to the hardware store on the corner and get some large screws," the intern suggested.

"Better get a screwdriver while you're at it," Kenyon suggested.

"Yeah, good idea."

Kenyon propped the rod back in place, taking some sour chewing gum out of his mouth and inserting it into the hole. He stood back and watched as the rod stayed in place this time. Then, without warning, a sharp knock sounded at the door.

"What did you forget now?" Kenyon yelled as he opened the front door.

"FBI? Internal Affairs maybe?" Fitz suggested with a sarcastic tone.

"Who wants to know?" Kenyon replied with equal amounts of indignation and embarrassment.

"Captain Stanley Fitzgerald, 1st Precinct," Fitz replied flashing his gold shield with the letters NYPD brazen across the top.

"I'm sorry Captain...Special Agent Joel Kenyon, Diplomatic Security Service," he replied as the two exchanged a strong handshake.

"Inventive...I'll give you that," the NYPD detective said as he strolled into the dingy flat, looking it over from top to bottom.

"Can I help you in any way?"

"You keeping an eye on our friends across the street?"

"You could say that. This *is* a matter of diplomatic security..."

"Yeah...right," Fitz replied with a smile. "I'm looking for a missing woman. You may have seen her enter and leave some time this past Monday night," Fitz showed the agent a picture of Zoë.

"Zoë Greene, the actress. Yeah, we had her going in at around 10:00 PM, then she left at 11:30 or so."

"Did she come back?" Fitz asked.

"I left at midnight. Give me a second," Kenyon said as he thumbed through a DSS surveillance log. "Nope, no record. That was the last time we tracked her. She's off the map after that."

"Thanks Agent Kenyon," Fitz said, running his finger over the surveillance equipment at the window. "So, what do you think you're going to get from this? Do you really think they are going to operate out in the open?"

"You haven't seen this guy's FBI file."

"Hell, Agent, *I've* got an FBI file."

"Yeah, but yours doesn't fill a file cabinet," Kenyon responded.

"Not yet anyway," Fitz quipped, smiling again. "This is Roman we're talking about here, right?"

"Not officially of course."

"Right."

"They've had two significant sit-downs in the last three days. Did you know that?"

"I did," Fitz replied, more smugly this time. "Agent Kenyon, have you ever seen the movie *The Hunt For Red October*?"

"Of course. It's a classic."

"You remember the part where Jack Ryan was trying to convince the Navy commander that Sean Connery's character, the Russian sub captain, was trying to defect?"

"Yeah, they were on a U.S. sub or something."

"Think of me as your Jack Ryan, Commander."

"What are you trying to say?"

"Roman Sabarese is trying to defect and he plans to dismantle the entire infrastructure of his father's organization in the process."

"You can't be…"

"Serious?" Fitz cut him off. "I have information that would indicate that he's making his boys stand out."

"Stand out?"

"It means he's forcing them to stand on their own…without his protection or any financial obligations to the family."

"So what do you recommend, Captain?" Kenyon asked.

"Sit back and watch. And maybe, stay the hell out of his way."

"That's going to be hard to do."

"There's more to this story than I think you know."

"Isn't there always?" Kenyon replied as his intern made his way through the front door, trying to juggle a bag of supplies from the hardware store, some donuts and two coffees.

"This isn't the place. Look, are you working the big party tomorrow?"

"Of course…Times Square," Kenyon advised.

"How convenient, me too. Let's hook up around eleven or so. Here's my card and I jotted my cell number on the back."

Chapter 35

Friday, December 31st
6:40 AM
17 hours, 20 minutes left

For Fitz the sixth floor of New York Methodist Hospital was starting to become his personal hell. The fact that most of the other patients on the sixth felt the same way was irrelevant. He had tried to maintain a good attitude about his ordeal but the time and discomfort were starting to weight heavy on his testament.

He sat reclining in a heavily padded hospital chair, trying to make himself as comfortable as possible. Remarkably, a new nursing student had gotten access to one of the veins in his arm on the second stick. As the poisonous chemicals flowed into his system, he could feel the flushness come over his body. Sweat formed on his forehead and before long the thin white undershirt he was wearing was moist with perspiration. Had he been counting, he would have known that this was the sixty-fourth treatment in thirty weeks. For some reason though, this time felt different.

"Excuse me," Fitz asked a passing nurse. "Do you know where Maria Gomez is?"

"Sorry, I don't. She works in the ER, right?"

"Yes ma'am."

"I heard they were working a bad traffic accident down there, a real pileup. She might be busy with that. Do you want me to call her?"

"No, don't bother. It'll be okay," he replied sitting back, trying to ignore the uneasiness he was feeling.

Ten minutes later Fitz could barely open his eyes.

"Call Maria…please," he muttered as one of the oncology nurses passed.

"Oh honey. You'll be okay," the busy woman replied.

"No…something's wrong."

"Let me get a blood pressure. You do look a bit ashen," the nurse said as she rolled a portable vital machine over and attached a Velcro blood pressure cuff.

In the emergency room the day shift nurses had just finished cleaning up after a busy morning. A six-car traffic accident had netted them ten patients, all of whom would live to see another day. It was a round of successes, one after the other for the crew of fourteen nurses, three physicians and eleven medical techs.

Maria Gomez finished entering her last bit of patient notes as the discussion at the nurses' station turned towards lunch.

"So what are we having?" Maria asked.

"I don't care. I'm starving," one of the techs replied.

"It's been a good morning. You fly and the department's going to buy. Deal?" Maria offered as the tech grabbed her purse and keys. Then, as Maria signed her name and date to the last patient's chart, a shrill beep came over the ceiling-mounted intercom system.

"ER supervisor to oncology – ER supervisor to oncology – STAT!"

As she exited the elevator two minutes later on the sixth floor and entered the oncology unit, the seasoned nurse stopped and gasped. Staff members were scurrying about as Fitz's limp arm dangled down from the recliner he was seated in.

"He's crashing!" one of the nurses yelled. "BP is sixty over thirty and falling fast!"

"Let me in," Maria ordered, making a path through the people that surrounded Fitz's unconscious body. "Stop the flow!"

"But..." one of the nurse's objected.

"Just do it!" she yelled. "Prep a bag of lactated ringers."

"I don't..." the lead nurse tried to interject.

"Just do it and page Doctor Bensualli," Maria insisted, ripping out the line supplying the chemo to her patient's veins. She looked over at the cardiac monitor that was connected to the three wires extending from some adhesive pads that were applied to Fitz's chest.

"You see this rhythm people?!" Maria said in an irate tone. "This is ST elevation. This means he's drying out. We need fluid now."

Maria grabbed the bag of lactated ringers, a solution of water and vital electrolytes. After plugging the clear plastic tubing into Fitz's IV catheter, she took her hands and squeezed the bag, pushing the fluid into her dehydrated patient.

"Kidney cancer! What part of renal dehydration don't you people understand?"

"I'm sorry," the lead nurse said with tears in her eyes. "Tell it to him sweetheart. Medical errors kill over ninety-eight thousand patients every year in this country. Just be glad he's not going to be one of them," Maria added as Fitz lifted an arm in a recovering and confused state.

"What happened?" he mumbled. "Where am I? Where's Maria?"

"I'm right here love. Everything's going to be okay. You got a little thirsty," his nurse said as she took a damp washcloth and wiped his forehead. "You're not getting out of our date that easily mister."

Fitz looked up and said in a groggy voice, "that's not my style."

"Have you been hydrating properly?" Maria asked.

"Six pack of Gatorade everyday."

"That's the problem with this type of chemo, especially with renal patients. It tends to dry you out," Maria explained. "Next time we need to hook you up to a cocktail of D5W, okay?"

"Whatever you say."

"Good. I'm glad you're coming to your senses and finally agreeing with me. I've got a call into Dr. Bensualli and it's my opinion that we need to keep you here for a couple of days."

"No way. I'm sorry but I've got mandatory duty tonight."

"I'm afraid that's out of the question," Maria insisted.

"Sorry Maria. Pump me up. I've got to walk out of this place in an hour."

"Fitz...what the hell am I going to do with you?"

"Hold that thought. This time tomorrow we're getting together for lunch, remember?"

"How could I forget? Just be careful tonight and take in plenty of fluids."

"I promise, doctor."

"Doctor? Please! I work for a living dear."

Chapter 36

8:11 AM
15 hours, 49 minutes left

Nello and Max got the office ready. Roman had kept a bank quality money counter in a cabinet above the manager's desk. Now it was plugged in, cleaned and ready for a grueling day of adding up all the cash that was to come to them from the six Sabarese captains. On an adjacent credenza between a copy machine and a computer printer, the two had laid out neat stacks of paper money straps in piles for fives, tens, twenties, fifties and hundred dollar bills. When the captain's payments arrived, most of the cash would be bound with simple rubber bands or in large manila envelopes and would most likely come in all denominations. It was imperative that all the money be counted, bound and ready for the next stage.

Once the deposit was ready it would be ferried to the airport at Teterboro, New Jersey. From there, it would be loaded onto a private plane and flown directly to the Scotia Bank in Georgetown, the capital of the Cayman Islands. Despite the holiday, a special envoy from Scotia Bank would accept the cash and credit a specially marked account.

"I guess I'm welcoming the new year down south," Max said.

An hour later a truck from Hudson Produce Company delivered the first of six planned shipments for the day from Big John Ciasuli. The white cube van that was painted with murals of various fruits and vegetables backed into the tight alley with its backup alarm echoing between the brick walls. Nello opened the back of the restaurant as he waved the reversing truck back to the open double doors, flush with the wall. Inside, Bones rolled the truck's rear door up into the vehicle's ceiling and unloaded six duffle bags into the storage rooms behind them. From there Nello and Max carried the bags into the office and started the counting phase of the delivery.

Over the next six hours, the process was to be repeated another five times. Everything was running smoothly until Bones showed up empty handed on the sixth run.

"What do you mean he's bringing it himself?" Nello questioned.

"Gino said he preferred to do it this way," Bones answered.

* * *

Roman sat in the bar and reminded himself what a good idea it was to close the restaurant for the entire weekend. Scores of hyper-enthusiastic tourists roamed the streets outside like zombies in a bad horror film. As he sipped his coffee, the cell phone in his pocket began to ring.

"Yeah," he answered.

"It's Big John. I got that information you wanted."

"What's the deal?"

"We got a kid who works over at *The Observer*. He's into us for a few bucks so he was real free with the information. Seems the tip about Zoë's disappearance came from, and I'll quote, *a wise guy who lives in Englewood and drives a new black Mercedes.*"

"Thanks Johnny. Delivery got here by the way. I want to thank you for following through with this."

"Hey, real friends never part brother. If you need anything, you know who to call."

"Thanks again," Roman finished as his cell phone beeped, ending the call. A few seconds later Nello joined him in the bar.

"I think we've got a problem with our friend in Jersey."

"You don't know the half of it…"

"What now?"

"This last story in the *Observer*…"

"No…"

"Gino leaked it."

"That little mother fu…"

"Hold that thought."

* * *

A white Dodge Maxi van with diplomatic plates and dark tinted windows had been loaded in the back alley of the restaurant with twenty-six duffle bags that had been segregated into denominations. Nello and Bones drove the van while Max followed in his XJ-6 Jaguar. Traffic off the island was heavy, but not nearly as bad as the bumper-to-bumper lines of partygoers that were waiting to get into Manhattan. After Bones navigated through the Lincoln Tunnel, the two cars made up their time, pulling into the entrance of Teterboro just before 2:00 PM.

The building that housed Executive Air Services was located amidst a long row of indiscriminant hangars. Bones drove into the only open door and parked next to a blue and white Israeli-built Jet Commander. The twin-engine aircraft wasn't the fastest or the most luxurious, but the reliability of the high wing version couldn't be replicated.

The company's owner and chief pilot, Ralph Linez, greeted the two at the plane's boarding steps while Max parked his car outside.

"Where's Maxie?" the pilot asked.

"He's parking the car," Nello said as Max entered through a side door carrying a light jacket and an overnight bag.

"So, are we going to party like it's 1999?" Max yelled, surprising Linez.

"Maxie!"

"Ralphie my man," Max yelled back as the two embraced.

"So, did you pack your sun block brother?" the pilot asked.

"Got my swimsuit and SPF 35. I've got rabbi skin, remember?"

"You guys are killing me," Bones remarked, shaking his head.

"Sorry pal, but if your P.O. finds out you left the country you're going back for sure. Besides, didn't you surrender your passport like thirteen years ago?" Max reminded him.

"I got plans tonight anyway," Bones said.

"Big date?" Linez asked.

"Yeah, with a pizza from Marones," Nello added.

"Welcome to my world," Bones said.

"Let's get this van unloaded, then I think I've got something that'll cheer you up," Nello said.

It took over half an hour to transfer the nineteen bags to the waiting plane. Linez took his time tying the cash cargo in place with heavy ratchet straps. It was imperative that all the bags be stationary as a sudden shift in placement could translate to a shift in the plane's weight and balance, a situation that could prove disastrous, especially during the Jet Commander's takeoff and landing. In his earlier days, the Cuban born pilot made the majority of his money flying loads of cocaine and weed through the Florida Keys from South America and the Bahamas. He had seen too many planes like his end up in the surf because eager pilots didn't take the time to prepare the load they were carrying.

As Bones and Nello pulled out of the open hangar, Linez started his preflight check. Ten minutes later, the two General Electric turbo fans that were bolted to the plane's tail were whining up and creating a thrust that would push the micro jet skyward. In another twenty it was wheels up banking south towards the nineteenth parallel.

* * *

Roman's phone rang just as he was entering the men's room. It was just as well. The coffee he had been drinking all day was starting to take its toll on his bladder and the downstairs restroom was far away from everyone else.

"Yeah."

"Roman, it's Fitz."

"Hey man. How are things going on your side of the fence?"

"Not too good. Bad day and to top it off I got nothing on Zoe…I'm sorry."

"As her manager, Melanie notified NBC that she's down with the flu and won't be able to do tonight's countdown show."

"Tough break. It could have been some good exposure for her. I even hear Dick Clark is going to sit this one out and let the younger set take it."

"Things are changing Fitz."

"So, I got to ask. You on board with all this *tech killed the mob* stuff?"

"I think the mob killed itself. Sure technology helped but in the end, we were all to blame for its demise."

"We? You speak as though you're a part of this thing."

"Aren't I? As a good friend of mine always says: *perception is reality*."

"Good point."

"My question isn't what all the cameras and the wiretaps will do to the mob. My question is what it will do to society. If character is molded by what we do when no one is watching, then what happens when someone is *always* watching?" Roman asked, reflecting for a second that his best thoughts always did come while he was in the bathroom.

"I never thought of it that way."

"Character, Fitz, is like a muscle. It needs to be exercised."

"Roman…there's something I have to tell you."

"This doesn't sound good," Roman replied, zipping up his pants as he flushed the toilet.

"I always thought I would have time to make the case…something else would come to light and I could put it all together."

"What are you talking about Fitzgerald?"

"Gino Spazio…the day in the alley with Bettina. We got a partial print off the gun he left. Must have been a hole in the glove or something. Anyway, it was never enough to make a positive ID based on the fingerprint standards of our illustrious district attorney, but I knew. Word is Spazio popped his family cherry with Bettina…*your Bettina*. We know he did it and now you know he did it," Fitz said.

"Why are you telling me this?" Roman asked as he looked towards the bathroom's white tile floor.

"Ninety-eight thousand people die every year because of medical errors. This morning I came close to being one of them. I honestly don't know how much time I have left and I can't leave this world without this one issue being settled. Spazio stole from *both* of us, remember?"

"Every day. A night doesn't go by without my mind revisiting those memories."

"So then, that's it. I've done my part. It's in your hands now."

"Just like that?"

"What...you were waiting for an engraved invitation?"

Chapter 37

5:04 PM
6 hours, 56 minutes left

Pilot Ralph Linez radioed the Georgetown Tower as he entered his path for the plane's final approach to the tiny island airport. Hydraulic cylinders mounted into the Jet Commander's belly lowered the landing gear as Linez switched the plane's flaps to a down angle of twenty degrees. In the copilot's seat, Max Weintraub adjusted his seatbelt and placed a stick of gum into his mouth to help correct the imbalance of atmospheric pressure within his ears.

"Georgetown Tower, 875 Kilo, clear to land runway twenty-six. Proceed to Aztec Air taxiway 3B."

"Rodger Georgetown Tower, Runway twenty-six to taxiway 3B," Linez repeated.

As the Jet Commander pulled up to the Aztec hangar, he spun the nose gear to the right and parked the large plane in the designated visitor's spot. Then he applied the brake lock and shut down the twin turbo fans. Max unfastened his seatbelt as the engines wound down to a state of silence. In no time a small blue Toyota van pulled up to the resting plane while Max orchestrated the unloading. As the lawyer jumped into the passenger seat of the van, Linez secured his plane and paid for the fuel supply that would get them home on Sunday. A blond receptionist behind the counter attracted the pilot's complete attention as he counted out a stack of crisp hundred dollar bills with his mind on the upcoming night.

"So what are your plans for the big party tonight?" he asked, leaning on the counter in front of her.

"Some girlfriends and I are going over to the Palm Bay Club for drinks and some dancing."

"The Palm Bay Club? My buddy Max and I are staying at the Palm Bay Club."

"Well then…you'll have to buy a girl and her friends a round."

"Just one?" Linez answered with a coy smile.

"We'll see, cowboy."

As the pilot continued to flirt he was unable to see the blue Toyota van circle out of the Aztec parking lot and head down the row of hangars to Caribe Air at the end of the airport service road. The van's driver pulled up to a waiting Cessna Citation and in ten minutes Max had the twenty-six duffle bags loaded. He paid the van driver with ten hundred dollar bills, pulled the main door shut and as quickly as they landed, the Citation screamed down Cayman runway eight. Once airborne, the slim jet banked to the left and made a direct course for Sao Paulo, Brazil.

Two hours later pilot Ralph Linez laid on his bed in the hotel room, dialing the front desk.

"Max Weintraub's room please."

"I'm sorry but we don't have a Max Weintraub staying with us."

"You have to. We flew down here together."

"I'm sorry sir. Could he be registered under another name?"

"No, but if he does check in could you please have him call me?"

"Sure. Will do Mr. Linez."

* * *

Roman sat in the front passenger seat of his own truck while Nello drove. Bones sat in the backseat, trying to sneak a nap during their quick trip back to New Jersey. The mauve-colored Mercury Vapor lights that were spaced every twenty feet throughout the Lincoln Tunnel were mesmerizing, but Bones didn't need any help. Nello looked over at Roman with a smile as his partner started to snore. Unlike the rough ride of Bones' Ford Bronco, Roman's plush Chevy pickup absorbed all the road's imperfections like a new Cadillac. As the three cleared the end of the tunnel, the sun was starting to set ahead in an explosion of orange and pink light that splintered through the different buildings of Jersey City. Behind them, New York became enveloped in darkness as the biggest party in history was about to begin.

"You don't have to do this you know," Nello offered.

"Some things are just inevitable," Roman replied.

From Interstate 495, Nello took a ramp north and entered the New Jersey Turnpike, which doubled as the state's portion of Interstate 95. In no time they were headed towards the trendy elite neighborhood of Englewood and the home of Gino Spazio.

Twenty-five minutes later, the burgundy truck pulled into the dark circular drive of Gino's eighty-seven-hundred-foot mansion and parked behind a new black Mercedes coupe. The home had been a point of contention between Ray Senior and Gino from the start. The eldest Sabarese had argued that its opulence was prone to attract attention. The home was valued at just under three million and sat next door to an equally large palace that had been the previous home to actress Brooke Shields. "Senior don't got no room to talk," Gino would say, referencing his boss's own mansion on Staten Island.

As Roman and Nello went to the front door, Bones slipped through a side gate to the back entrance, activating a high intensity motion light in the process. Once they knew he was in place, Roman depressed a button that sent a series of chimes throughout the immense interior. Then Nello peered through a tall window that was adjacent to the twelve-foot-high main entry.

"Just a second," came a voice from inside, muffled by the home's insulation.

"It's him," Nello whispered as Gino looked through the small peephole in the center of the massive wooden door.

"Shit!" Gino whispered as though the door would insulate his words.

The two continued to stand at the door while Gino, with wet hair and wearing a silk bathrobe, danced around the inside of the door in a panic. And then they heard it.

"Open the fuckin' door Gino. Who do you think you are keeping Roman waiting like this?" Bones ordered from inside the home as Gino unlocked the deadbolt and apologized.

"Roman, I didn't know it was you. I was in the shower," he said pointing to his hair and robe. "Gotta meet the wife and kid in Wayne for a big party."

"This is some place you got here Gino," Roman said looking up at the high ceilings and an ornate chandelier that hung in front of a tall circular staircase.

"We got a problem Gino," Nello announced.

"What?"

"The money never arrived," Roman announced.

"I know. It's crazy. Too much going on at once. Let's finish the deal on Monday, okay?"

"Not okay Gino. The plane's already left."

"Roman, come on."

"Let's go to little Gino's room and make good," Nello said.

"What?"

"Come on Gino, we all know about the safe in your kid's room. Don't be an asshole."

"Okay, but I don't have that kid of cash here," Gino said, shaking as he spoke.

"Consider it a down payment," Roman reasoned.

As the four went up the curved staircase, Bones looked at the hundred or so lights on the chandelier. "I could get used to this," he commented, nodding his head.

"We were thinking about downsizing actually," Gino said.

"Really?" Roman asked.

"Yeah, I was thinking about all that your dad said in the past and he's right. It's too much. The wife is going to be disappointed."

"Sorry to hear it," Roman responded sarcastically.

As they crested the last step, Gino led them to his son's room. It was cluttered with toys, dirty clothes, and junk food wrappers. In the back of the room was a door that led to a large walk-in closet, in the back of which sat a four-foot-high shoe organizer. Gino pushed it aside to reveal a large in-wall safe.

"That's what I'm talking about," Bones said as Gino got down on his knees and entered a code into a keypad that was mounted on the front.

"12345?" Nello repeated. "That's your security code? Really Gino?"

"I forget shit Nello. I got a lot on my mind."

As the door swung open, all four looked in as Roman pulled a double handled ripcord from his pocket. He put the handles in both hands and looped the cord over Gino's head as the frigid man looked forward, unaware of what his fate was about to hold. Roman snapped the cord tight, jerking the man to his feet.

"Where's Zoë you prick!" Roman demanded.

"What are you talking about?" Gino spit his words, trying to gasp for air as Roman pulled tighter.

"You killed Bettina Cooper, *my* Bettina. Senior ordered that you make the whole package disappear," Roman yelled. "And then you figured out that Zoë survived and you couldn't live with that, could you."

"I saw to it myself Roman. Both are dead. I'm sorry! It was an order. I was just doing…"

"I got my orders too, asshole," Roman announced as he pulled the cord as tight as he could, squeezing Gino's neck and crushing his windpipe in the process. The scared little man fell limp as Roman continued to pull even tighter and a tear fell from his left eye. Nello patted Roman on the shoulder as he let go. Gino fell to the floor, completed, unconscious and breathless as Roman looked down at his hands. They were shaking. Then he looked down at Gino who was lying on the floor in a still state.

"Get that rug," Nello ordered as Bones went back into the kid's room from the closet and retrieved a multicolored piece of carpet that had pictures of trucks, planes and boats designed into it. "Wrap him up."

Nello then got down on his knees and emptied the contents of the safe.

"About a hundred K in cash…Roman!"

"What? Roman responded, distracted by his own actions.

"We've got a hundred K and another three mil in bearer bonds. Jackpot!"

"Good. They're better than cash," Roman said slowly. "Take it all and put everything else in place and let's get the hell out of here."

Roman took the money and bearer bonds while Bones and Nello carried Gino, rolled in his son's rug, on their shoulders down the winding staircase. The three and their cargo made it to the front door as Roman looked for the keys to Gino's new black Mercedes. In a decorative tray sitting on a table in the foyer was a key ring with something that caught his eye. Attached to a short gold chain that held the dozen or so keys was a gold ring. It had a large diamond mounted in the center with a green gem on either side of the main stone. Roman recognized it immediately. It was his grandmother's ring, the same one he gave to Bettina twenty-five years before for their engagement. *He made a damn keychain out of it,* Roman thought to himself with disgust as he removed the ring from the rest of the keys.

In ten minutes, the house was locked and the three, with their new cargo, were headed back into the city. Earlier that evening the radio had reported that all the south city accesses were backed up deep into New Jersey. Nello drove Roman in the truck and Bones took Gino's Mercedes with his lifeless body wrapped in a rug and stowed neatly in the trunk. Nello led the way, heading east on Interstate 95 into Harlem. As they landed on the island a police roadblock made for a few minutes of anxiety.

A long line of road cones and bright amber flares divided the traffic into two lanes with trucks and vans going one way and all other automotive traffic going the other. After being flagged over, an NYPD officer approached Nello, who had his license and registration ready.

"Everything okay officer?" Nello asked.

"Yes sir. Just a security precaution. We are checking all large vehicles entering the city…what with the big celebration and all. Can't be too careful."

"We agree. Whatever we can do to help."

"Sir, if you could just open the back tailgate and tarp of the truck for me and then you can be on your way."

"Sure officer," Nello replied as he got out and grabbed the rear latch, watching Bones pass in the car lane a hundred feet away. With the bed empty and nothing else present to raise the officer's suspicion, he let the two pass. As they drove off with the checkpoint in their rearview mirror Roman's phone began to ring.

"Get that, will ya?" Roman asked.

"Hello," Nello answered.

"Roman? It's Ralph Linez."

"No Ralph. It's Nello. Roman's busy right now," he advised as he whispered over to Roman. "Ralph…the pilot."

"Something's not right Nello."

"What do you mean? Where's Max?"

"Max has disappeared."

"It's a small island. How could he just disappear?"

"He never showed up at the hotel. I waited. Now I got some guy who says Max gave me the switch and boarded another plane a few hours ago. Nello…he's got the cash."

"Let me call you back. Enjoy your evening and we'll get back to you," Nello finished as he pressed the *end* button.

"Don't tell me," Roman said with a sigh.

"I guess everyone's got their price," Nello said.

"Even you?"

"Of course…but don't worry. You can't afford it," Nello said as he patted Roman on the shoulder. "Besides, your Dubai project is going to make me a rich man."

"Good thing Max didn't have any control over that," Roman conceded.

"It's not been a good day for you."

"Yeah. And right now all I can think about is one thing..."

"We'll find her," Nello reassured.

"That's something about Max. I guess the pressure just got to him. Divorce can do crazy things to people."

"It's still a lot of money."

"It wasn't ours. That was my father's deal and Max was his boy. What comes around goes around."

"Actually, I think it's what goes around comes around."

"I like my way better."

"So what now?"

"You get to tell my father."

"Oh, that's not going to happen."

"Okay tough guy."

"Tell me Roman...how did it all end up like this?"

"It's evolution. Technology killed this thing, and to be truthful, I'm not so sad. Most revere it, but I know it better than most. It's a cult and it destroys lives."

* * *

The black Mercedes was the first to make it to a depressed street in Harlem. Scores of partiers stood on the street downing bottles of beer and other alcohol from paper bags. It was there that Bones parked the Mercedes with the key in the ignition. It was anyone's guess, considering the volatility of the night, where Gino and his precious car would end up, and whose fingerprints and DNA would grace the interior. From there the three rode Roman's truck down Harlem River Drive to Park and south to Roman's apartment.

Nello and Bones jumped the subway with one headed home to his wife in the Village and the other to his invalid mother in Queens.

As the doorman at 450 Park Avenue started to open the large glass entry pane, Roman looked at him with weary eyes.

"You okay Mr. Sabarese?"

"Yeah, hey I think I'll walk for a while," he replied as he headed south towards Saint Bartholomew's Church at 50th Street. It had been seven years since he had seen the inside of the church that most commonly called Saint Bart's. The occasion was for his older brother Ray Junior's funeral. Since the restaurant was open on Saturdays and Sundays he didn't have the time to attend regular services, although he and his father were both officially members of the Episcopal parish that was founded in 1835.

At the main entrance he opened the ornate door that was twelve-feet-tall and carved from a single piece of oak wood. There was no expense spared by the congregation over the years to make this a monumental house of worship not only to God, but also to the amalgamated achievements of the church itself. Inside, scores of candles burned on one side as tourists flashed strobes from assorted cameras, trying to preserve their memory of the beautiful sanctuary. As they continued, the flashes bounced off the sixty-foot-high ceilings and intricately decorated walls. Huge murals covered the expansive masonry that was trimmed with more ornate stone, most of which had been constructed long before the turn of the *last* century.

Roman walked down past the long wooden pews towards the altar at the front. Confession wasn't his style. He didn't think much of the priests and, while he wasn't overly religious, he did believe that one could connect directly with God and do so without the assistance of a priest, pastor or any other well-paid religious professional.

"You can run from the law, you can run from your wives, but you can't run from God," his father used to say. That was one of his older saying though; long before he took over La Trattoria and turned it into Evangeline's and long before losing Bettina. It was at this very point, with less than four hours left in the closing millennium, that he accepted the fact that no more options remained. He was a man that had been accustomed to being in control and creating his own destiny and now someone that was a pinnacle in his life, Zoë, was gone, and every hour that passed seemed to seal that terrible fact.

Roman closed his eyes as he knelt at the church's altar. "God, please forgive me for what I've done," he pleaded. "I have caused so much pain to so many and tonight, I've taken another's life. Please return this precious child. I will give anything to have her back and safe…*anything*," he opened his eyes while tapping the four corners of the cross on his chest. As he did, a side door to the sanctuary opened and a brief gust of cold wind entered, blowing out several rows of burning candles. In its wake hundreds of small smoke trails floated into the air.

A half hour later and completely exhausted, Roman sat on his couch with the TV off and Trooper biting at his feet. He had killed before but that was different. It was war and his enemy was just as intent on killing him. In Vietnam he had thirty-four confirmed kills, more than the average and not enough, according to his own standards. With scores of different thoughts going through his mind, Roman drifted off to sleep, taking with him the emotional baggage he had carried most of the day.

Chapter 38

9:49 PM
2 hours, 11 minutes left

She had been the daughter of a single mother from Brooklyn, a woman of means who, as she understood it, needed a change and the Manhattan lifestyle and child to share it with seemed like the right thing to fill a huge hole in her heart. Nothing was as she had expected it to be. The only reason Zoë embarked on her quest was to get a closer look at someone she had trusted for so many years. Now she was torn and feeling guilty about questioning Roman in the first place. As it turned out, he had been legitimate all along and to make matters worse, he too was a victim, losing his love Bettina. *But what about the stories?* she reasoned. *How could papers like The Observer print such an article without any proof?*

Zoë grabbed the handle and pulled the top drawer open. It slid forward to reveal a series of files and a clear plastic envelope with a stack of what appeared to be old birthday cards. In bold letters the tab read *EVANGELINE.* Not Evangeline's, as in the restaurant, but Evangeline, the person. *Would this unlock the mystery behind Roman's fractured spirit?* she thought as she opened the first birthday card. It was the type that had a paper wheel attached to the inside of the front flap so the sender could rotate it to reveal the recipient's celebrated age, five, six or seven. The wheel was fastened in place by a metal rivet that had been long rusted in place by the extreme moisture in the sub-basement. A bright pink number seven had been frozen, visible through a square cutout in the front flap of the card. Inside was a handwritten note, and Zoë recognized the style.

My dearest Evangeline,
2/15/81

Today is your birthday and I am secure knowing that you are in good hands and probably having the time of your life. I hope you enjoy the stuffed Amish bunny. My mother, your grandmother, used to collect them and I wanted you to have a piece of her with you at all times.

I'm writing this because a friend said it would be healthy, although I know you will never be able to read it. The importance of releasing these feelings is paramount to me right now.

It is a daily struggle for me to fight the consumption of what my anger has become. The atrocities that have been committed against you and your mother are, for lack of a better term, unforgivable. I want you to know that I take full responsibility for causing this chain of events that have ended with such death and despair.

Know that you were conceived out of a tremendous amount of love between your mother and I. You were then subsequently born into immediate tragedy. As you live your life, I hope and pray that you get the love and safety you deserve on a daily basis. Many have fought and sacrificed to make your life possible.

Daddy

Daddy...the word struck her like a ton of bricks, almost as much as the handwriting. She had worked at the restaurant for almost five years. In the end she was tending to the meat of the business, crunching numbers, calculating payroll and reading many of Roman's instructions, his *handwritten* instructions. *Roman wrote this letter.* To make things more confusing, the date of the kid's birthday, *Evangeline's* birthday, was February 15th. *That's my birthday,* she thought as her mind made a split-second calculation. *Seven years old in 1981 would mean...*Zoë dropped the letter as she put a hand to her mouth.

After a moment of thought, she began to claw at the papers and files in the drawer until she came across two birth certificates, identical in almost every way. The date, time, and place all coincided with the other. The names, however, were different. Bettina Cooper became Melanie Greene, Roman Sabarese became Horace Greene, and the most striking to her, Evangeline Sabarese became Zoë Greene.

The single Jewish mother who moved to the East Village from Brooklyn was not her biological mother. For Zoë, that left one mounting question: Who was? Melanie was her natural mother she immediately conceded, a benefactor of love and devotion that she had never seen in the mother-daughter relationships of her close friends. It began to haunt her. *Who was Bettina? My mother? Did she gave birth to me? How? What were the circumstances?* For years she believed that her father had been killed before she was born. It's the story Melanie had repeated. She was, after all, white and black, both and neither, the product of a mixed relationship. To think about it made her cry.

Melanie had her baggage to deal with. Zoë could see the glares of those that cast their judgmental stares at them. It was bad enough that her mother was unwed, a scenario made worse with the idea that her child's father had been of color and was now gone. "That's what black men do," people would say. And their inability to keep Zoë's young mind out of earshot were of no concern to them. The fact that Melanie sacrificed her standing in the community and the endless superficial friendships that she could have had, all for her child's benefit, a child that was not biologically hers, squelched all desires for Zoë to look any further. Had she grown up in the late nineties instead of the seventies and eighties it might not have been so bad, but it was what it was and even in a cosmopolitan area like New York, prejudices ran deep. Melanie may have not been her biological mother, but she was her natural one, a natural in deed.

* * *

High tides were not uncommon for this part of the country and certainly not uncommon for New York. What was unusual was to have such a tide coincide with an abnormally low-pressure weather system that was circled by a series of high ones. Simply put, with all the high pressure acting on the region's seawater pushing it down, and the low system over New York allowing it to rise, the stage had been set for the New Year tide to be the highest in forty-seven years. In that time improvements to the city's subway system, and more specifically the Tribeca lines, had taken place. A new upgraded tunnel, new platform and stronger rails were just some of the improvements that had been completed. One of the legs that received a new tube, as it was called, was a stretch of line that ran parallel and twenty feet under the surface of Greenwich Street and right under Evangeline's.

As the water rose from the unusual tide, pressure built against the concrete walls of the main train tubes that were fifteen feet in diameter. Inch-by-inch, as the seawater flowed back from New York Harbor and collided with the southward flow of the Hudson, it infiltrated deeper into the aquifer of lower Manhattan. As the outer sea pressure increased, the level of saturation also increased until the walls of the train tube became a dam, a structure they were not designed to be. At first there was a constant dripping and then a small stream. At the Red Line branch just under Greenwich Street, the first wall gave way as the water pressure equalized with the subterranean air space, flooding the subway tunnel. As more water entered and the level rose, so did the pressure against the wall that separated the train tube from the sub-basement of Evangeline's until a portion of that wall also failed and acrid seawater poured into the concrete floor, engulfing the old rusty freezer.

Zoë heard the noise at first. Her initial thought was that someone had come back down to the sub-basement.

"Hey!" she yelled. "Help! Please!"

There was no response and then she felt it. Water started to flow inside the freezer, funneling through the rusty holes and cracks at the box's base. The frigid water lapped over her bare feet in a matter of seconds and started to rise quickly.

"Help!" she screamed. "HEEEEELP!"

In less than a minute the water was up to her knees as she heard the sump pump activate. It ran for five minutes before blowing a circuit in the fuse box located a floor above.

Thoughts began to cycle through her frightened mind. *Not now!*

* * *

An alarm sounded inside New York's Metro Transit Hub. On the wall and before a series of consoles was a backlit acrylic screen with the city's grid of tracks and stations labeled in black and red. Much to the surprise of the personnel of eight that were manning the different computer consoles, the section marked *Redline / Greenwich Branch* was flashing with its own series of backlit amber lights.

"Polarity alarm on Greenwich Red," one of the men yelled out.

"What do you think Chief?"

"It's this damn tide. Water's rising fast. It's probably flooding the tube."

Twenty minutes later a crew from train maintenance services climbed down from the Chambers Street station platform with flashlights that bounded their erratic beams down the dark tunnel that disappeared in total darkness. The power had been disconnected to the tracks on this leg and all trains had been stopped. Swarms of stranded inpatient commuters stood behind the men on the elevated platform watching and wondering when they would be connected with a train. As the men proceeded down the tracks, their lights caught a glimpse of small packs of rats that were scurrying in the opposite directions.

"That's not good," one of the inspectors said.

The decline approached thirty degrees as the tunnel entered the deepest portion of the city's train line. As they rounded bend in the tunnel they could see what the problem was. Water was gushing in through a series of cracks in the stone wall. The tide had risen considerably in the last hour and wasn't expected to crest for another ninety minutes.

"It's a damned full moon. That, and a low pressure system," one of the men remarked. "We might have to shut down this leg for a while," he continued, shining his light at the iron tracks that descended into and below the surface of the water ahead.

"And that's seawater. The salt's gonna eat this metal alive."

* * *

She had been confined for almost two days and now Zoë heard the muffled voices through the wall. They were close and she knew it. The water was rising fast and this was her only chance.

"Hey!" she yelled. "I'm in here! Help!" she continued as she began hitting the inside of the freezer.

"Help! Please!" she cried with tears of frustration.

The water was cold and had risen to her waist. She sloshed around in a panic as the frigid liquid bubbled up around her. As it rose, she could feel her feet lifting off the wooden floor as her body became buoyant. In her haste, she splashed water on the hot light bulb that was now at her head. It exploded with a shower of glass and sparks, leaving her in a state of cold, bitter darkness.

* * *

"You hear that?" one of the engineers asked.

"All I hear are those thousand or so assholes we left back on the platform."

"You can't be mad at them. They just want to get home for New Year's."

"Regardless, we need to get some pumps down here and fast."

"We will need to get the platform cleared first. Those pumps throw a lot of carbon monoxide."

"Shit. So much for watching the ball drop tonight guys," the realist in the group concluded as the men returned to the station.

Chapter 39

11:06 PM
54 minutes left

Bones sat in his favorite easy chair. It had belonged to his dad. His mom had been bathed by the visiting nurse and put to bed. The rest of the evening was his. He grabbed the remote control and popped open a cold bottle of Heineken. It was a treat, a reward to himself for his week of hard work. For his efforts, Nello had paid him well. It was enough money to stock his mother's twenty year old refrigerator with beer and steaks, put gas in the Bronco and save a substantial sum for the future. As he thumbed through the channels, the ex-con thought it was amazing that so many choices had evolved since he had left for prison in 1986. After narrowing down his options, he settled on an episode of *Miami Vice* that was airing on an all night outlet called *TV Land Network*. Ironically, it was the same episode that had aired on NBC the week after he left for Terre Haute. It was as though he was picking up where he had left off, a warm home, food in the fridge, a cold bottle of beer in his hand and money in his pocket. *Life was good,* he thought.

As the night progressed, Bones drifted off to sleep. The episode of *Miami Vice* had been part of an all night marathon and he was anxious to see as much as he could. The previous long nights were starting to take their toll though, and he was fast asleep by the third rerun. Everything was quiet with the exception of the noise coming from the TV. The comfortably dressed Crockett and Tubbs raced through the pastel streets of Miami in their white Ferrari Testarossa as the melody of a techno-hit popular for 1986 played in the background. Then, a noise from the rear of the ground floor apartment startled him from his sleep. It sounded like some trashcans falling over and Bones sat up straight, orienting himself to his conscious surroundings. He was not yet used to waking up in any other space than his eight-by-six-foot cell. It had been the routine for thirteen long years. The bright vision of his mother's living room was a relief and the tired man started to doze off again when he heard something even more startling, the muffled squawk of a police radio. Now he was scared. Bones shot up out of his chair and made his way to the back window, peering through the white translucent curtains. Everything outside was quiet, even the neighbor's dog that stayed penned up by his parked Bronco. A soft snow was starting to fall and it was at that point that Tommy T-Bone Bonatrelli had decided he was hearing things. He shook his head and headed for the easy chair.

Suddenly, three sharp knocks sounded at his mother's front door. Bones raced back to the curtains. Standing in front of his Bronco were two uniformed officers holding the dog that was kept in the pen.

"T-Bone? Thomas Bonatrelli? This is Sergeant Will Peterson with the New Jersey State Patrol. We need to talk."

Bones quietly reached for his gun as a tall shadow passed his window. *This was no talk*, he surmised. They came and they brought back up. That only meant one thing: he was going away.

His week of misdeeds must have, in some miraculous way, caught up with him and done so a lot quicker than he could have ever imagined.

"Hey Bones, it's me, Jim from BOP. Come on man, open up?" his federal probation officer asked.

As quietly as possible the tired man made his way upstairs to where his invalid mother was sleeping. He cracked open the door and watched her breathe, like a parent of a newborn staring down at a crib. The slow hiss of flowing oxygen was the only sound that filled the warm room beyond her soft breaths. He edged closer and bent down, giving her a soft kiss on the forehead.

Bang Bang Bang

"Come on Mr. Bonatrelli. This is only going to make things hard on all of us," a voice yelled from the back door stoop.

As the men continued to knock, Bones went into the kitchen and retrieved another cold bottle of beer. He sat back in his easy chair and turned the volume on the TV up all the way. More throbbing electronic music blared as the salt and pepper team from Miami interrogated a suspected drug dealer. Then, as though he had rehearsed it a hundred times, he took his Colt .45 and pointed it at the door and waited a few seconds. As a tear rolled down his face and with the wolves at the back door, he took the gun into his own mouth and pulled the trigger.

Chapter 40

11:23 PM
37 minutes left

The order had been given ninety minutes before to close Time Square. A record sum had amassed in and around the iconic hotspot as a myriad of music acts continued, each one vying to take the center stage of attention for the capital event, the changing of a millennium.

While the temperature should have been hovering just above thirty-one degrees, body heat and warm breath had added a level of ambient heat to the temperature on the square to almost fifty. The NYPD estimated the headcount at just over eight hundred thousand and uniformed officers had sealed the multiple streets and avenues that fed the area. Wooden barricades painted blue and white had been slid across the ice and snow, much to the objection of those that didn't enter in time. Those who were blocked out though simply retreated to Central Park where another four stages had been set up in anticipation of the overwhelming crowd.

The attendance was unprecedented. Hotels were full throughout the city with private apartments renting for over two thousand dollars a night. Hotels were also full on Long Island and fifteen miles deep into New Jersey.

Despite a multitude of objections, every police officer was on duty and wearing a uniform. Fitz hadn't donned a set of blues since the last department funeral over three months before. His health issues and the subsequent chemotherapy had taken its toll. He was twenty-two pounds lighter and his once snug uniform now hung to him like a cheap suit on a wooden hanger. Still, he managed, tightening his belt to the last prong and wearing two undershirts. Fortunately his vest had adjustable Velcro straps that helped him achieve the customized fit he needed.

He looked over at the gyrating crowd adorned in bright sparkling *2000* faux eyeglasses as they followed the music of fem rocker Courtney Love, the front of a band called *Hole.*

"Oh make me over, I'm all I want to be. A walking study in demonology…" she belted out through the several skyscraper-style speakers that towered over the crowd as the beat bounced from the buildings that encompassed the world's most famous intersection.

"So what do you think? Kinda crazy…" one of Fitz's subordinates yelled over the noise.

"It's not exactly my kind of music, but hey, expecting Marvin on the big stage would have been a bit unrealistic," Fitz admitted as his cell phone started to ring.

"Captain Fitzgerald?" asked the voice on the other end as Fitz put a finger in one ear and the phone close to the other.

"Yes, go ahead," he yelled, competing with the noise of the event.

"This is dispatch at Yonkers 4th Precinct. I was told to transfer the message that a body has been found over here."

"Okay?" Fitz asked, puzzled by the dispatcher's statement.

"There was a liquor store holdup, high speed chase and the perp crashed into a building just south of Nepperhan Ave."

"Thank you, but I still don't under…"

"Captain, there was a body found in the trunk. It's one Gino Spazio sir. You were listed at the top of his file for contact and control," she explained. Fitz paused as he put the phone to his forehead.

"Yes. Thank you. Have a good night."

"Don't you want to…" she started to ask.

"That will be all. Thank you," he finished, depressing the *end* button on his cell phone. *It was done.*

One of the detectives put his hand on his boss's shoulder. "You okay?"

"Yeah, I'm fine," Fitz replied.

"You're not going to believe who just off-ed himself an hour before midnight," the detective announced with a handheld radio to his ear, listening closely to the NYPD iterant frequency.

"What now?"

"T-Bone…one of the Sabarese boys," the detective replied with a look of surprise. "Did it with the his own parole officer knocking on his mother's front door."

As the detective continued to listen, Fitz walked away, reaching into his coat pocket for his second cell phone, the prepaid one he used for his conversations with Roman. As he dialed the number, he thought twice about whether he should be the one to notify Bones' friend, especially during such a festive time. After a few minutes, he took the phone in his palm and dialed with his thumb. The phone rang for five cycles before going to the computer voice of Roman's voicemail system. A message, under the circumstances, was not warranted. He would try again as the night progressed.

* * *

Roman dreamed as his phone rang, unanswered, on the living room couch where he had left it. The dreams always took him back to that time and place.

It was the day after the most incredible night of her life. Bettina Cooper awoke, startled by the noise from the radiator in Roman's Brooklyn apartment. She looked over at his side of the bed but it was empty. A small felt box, an inch-squared, sat on top of his flat pillow.

"I'm not very good at this," Roman conceded, coming into the room with two cups of coffee.

"What's going on?" she asked, trying to position her pregnant frame in the bed.

He looked at her as she rolled over on her side and put a pillow between her legs. She was completely naked with a rich flannel blanket draped over her in a way that made her seem even sexier to him. At eight months, she felt consumed with her appearance, although she had gained very little extra weight. Bettina had managed to balance her eating with the demands of her gestation, something she had learned during the nutrition portion of her nurse's training.

"Are you sure about this?" she asked, grabbing the box.

"As sure as I've ever been."

"What about *them*?" she asked, pointing out the window.

"They'll get over it. I love you and they will too," he said smugly.

"I admire your naiveté but it's not that simple and you know it."

"Once they see that ring on your finger, they'll have to accept you. You will have my father's name and the respect that comes with it."

"A black woman with an Italian last name is just that. They will never be able to see past my skin."

"Just open it."

As she popped open the spring-loaded box, the light from the bedroom's window caught the diamond just right. To his luck, it glistened with a brilliance no jeweler could have replicated. Shards of light reflected in her big, bright eyes as a tear formed and trailed down her cheek.

"Roman, it's beautiful. All I can do is trust that you can make all of this work out."

"Our baby deserves a family, and a family is what it's going to get."

A flash of light filled the vision in his sleeping mind as the dream continued, taking him to the lime-tiled walls of the emergency room of Brooklyn Methodist.

"Mr. Sabarese," Junior Detective Stanley Fitzgerald called out.

"What's going on?"

"We need to talk."

"Someone said something about an accident. Is it my brother or dad? Tell me something..."

"Roman, my name is Stan Fitzgerald. I'm a detective with the 78th Precinct," the nervous policeman said, motioning him into an empty chapel. "It was no accident. Someone shot and killed your friend Bettina Cooper."

Roman tried to speak but nothing came out. Tears formed in his eyes as he looked back at the bearer of his worst news.

"Who...where?"

"We gave chase. The shooter also shot my partner and he got away. She was taking a shortcut through a dark alley on her way here."

"Can I see her?"

"I'm sorry man. That's not a good idea."

"Oh God no…" he cried, as heavier tears flowed down his face. "She was…"

"Pregnant. I know. When you're ready, we need to take a walk."

"What?"

Roman's next sequence took his mind through the long winding halls of the hospital. The fluid motion stopped as the dreamscape entered the front of a small exam room that was guarded by an NYPD uniformed police officer.

"Maria," Fitz said to a nurse that had her back to them. "This is the father."

She turned holding a newborn baby that was resting comfortably in her arms.

"You must be Roman," she guessed. "Bettina has told me so much about you. I'm so sorry dear."

Fitz guided the stunned dreamer into the room and closed the door behind them.

"I know a million things are going through your head right now Roman," Fitz said. "But we've got to act fast."

"What do you mean?" Roman replied, staring down at the baby.

"The reason we were following Bettina in the first place was because our unit had received a tip that a hit had been placed on her."

"What?! From who?" Roman replied with skeptical disbelief.

"I think you know the answer to that question."

"That's crazy. Sure he's disappointed but…this?"

"Roman, it was a professional hit. Who else having those connections would want a young innocent student nurse dead?" Fitz reasoned as Roman stood in silence, continuing to stare at the floor.

"The baby's in danger. Bettina didn't have any family. I'm it," Roman calculated.

"We have taken precautions," Fitz replied, pointing at the uniformed officer standing watch at the door.

"I need your help," Roman announced.

*   *   *

Back in the mayhem of Times Square, Fitz couldn't hear the ringing cell phone in his pocket but he felt the vibration.

"Captain Fitzgerald," he answered.

"Captain, it's Joel Kenyon, DSS."

"Joel, yes. Are you in the square?"

"I am. Where's a good place to meet?"

"There's a small temp office set up next to the Virgin Music Superstore. Can you be there in five minutes?"

"On my way."

The small enclave turned out to be the perfect buffer from the crowds and the noise. Fitz ducked in and grabbed another bottle of Gatorade from a cooler he had stashed there earlier as a uniformed officer tried to get his attention.

"Captain, I need to talk to…"

"Not now son. Give me ten minutes."

"Yes sir," the officer said as Special Agent Joel Kenyon entered the small office.

"Give us the room please," Fitz ordered as the three remaining officers left immediately.

"This is some crowd," Kenyon remarked.

"Wait another hour when their average blood alcohol levels are up another few points."

"So, what was it you wanted to tell me?"

"Can I call you Joel?"

"Sure."

"Joel, twenty-five years ago my partner Bill Stewart and I were working in the organized crime unit based out of Brooklyn. We had been running surveillance on a young woman by the name of Bettina Cooper. Cooper, you see, was Roman Sabarese's girlfriend...his pregnant girlfriend. We had information that Roman's father, Ray Senior, had green-lighted a hit on her."

"None of this is in his file."

"I know. Pay attention," Fitz said, taking a quick swig of Gatorade. "She had been walking to New York Methodist Hospital when she decided to take a shortcut between two large industrial buildings. While in an alley someone shot her. We later learned that the shooter was one Gino Spazio, a then *soldier* of Ray Sabarese Senior. Bettina was his pledge and he was made soon after."

"My God. Does Roman know?"

"He does now," Fitz replied. "Joel, after we heard the shot, Bill and I ran into the alley and immediately took fire. Bill took a shot to the head and was killed instantly."

"So this has become a personal issue for you. That explains a lot."

"It was a complex situation and we all had to act fast."

"Wow! I bet."

"No, you don't understand," Fitz explained. "Bettina took a shot to the head. She was gone, but when EMU got there, one of their medics decided to try and save the baby. She was over eight months along after all."

"Sounds like a long shot."

"Sometimes those are the best. They rushed Bettina to Methodist a few blocks away and took her into surgery. It was close but the baby survived."

"Roman's got a kid?"

"Yes, she was a beautiful baby girl. But there are only a handful of people who know this, and now you're part of the club."

"Where is she now?" Kenyon asked.

"Because of the obvious threat to her life we pulled some strings."

"We?"

"Roman, myself, Maria Gomez, the ER duty nurse who was also Bettina's instructor, and the widow of an old war buddy of Roman's, Melanie Greene."

"No…" the agent replied with a dropped jaw.

"Yes," Fitz affirmed.

"Zoë Greene is Roman Sabarese's daughter?" Kenyon replied with his eyes wide open.

"You're pretty quick for a fed, Joel!"

"With all the press, we just assumed they were an item."

"Press Joel? Is that what the bureau calls *The Observer*?"

"Okay, point taken."

"Roman knew Melanie pretty well. She was his only real connection to the life he left behind in Vietnam. She had been lonely and depressed, having lost her husband over there and it was at this point that Roman made a proposition. He would set them up, money, a brownstone in the city and anything else they needed so long as the baby's identity was kept a secret. They couldn't take the chance that Roman's father would take another shot at hurting her. This was Ray Senior's flesh and blood after all, in the form of a young black girl."

"Is this guy really that bigoted?"

"He killed his pregnant, soon to be daughter-in-law."

"Roman was going to marry her?"

"Proposed the night before she was killed. Took some balls and I give him credit for that. A bit naive though. Guess he thought they would just accept her. Got to tell you, he's never quite forgiven himself for that."

"So for twenty-five years…"

"It's been kept a secret. To make matters more complicated, five years ago the kid, on her own mind you, shows up at the restaurant looking for a job. One of the managers hired her, not knowing who she really was. It was a fluke…a coincidence."

"What you are telling me makes sense. And now she's missing you say, since Monday. But why was Zoë Green in the restaurant on Wednesday?"

"Go back. You said Wednesday?"

"Here…look at this," Kenyon said as he reached into a leather satchel and pulled out a thin notebook computer. After flipping the top up, the hard drive started to whine and a video played on cue in the center of the screen.

"That's Tommy Bonatrelli," Fitz said pointing at the table where Bones was feasting on a plate of veal parmigiana.

"T-bone, right?"

"Yes, and dead as of twenty minutes ago."

"What? How? Jesus…" Kenyon remarked as though he knew the guy other than as a peripheral target of his investigation.

"Apparent suicide. GSW to the head with his PO at the door."

"The guy hasn't been out of the pen a week."

"Tell me about it. This is the stuff they don't show you on TV."

"Here…" Kenyon interrupted as a person flashed in front of the camera seemingly unnoticed by anyone. "Let me freeze it."

"This was two days ago?" Fitz asked.

"Wednesday," Kenyon said as he manually advanced the video, frame by frame, showing a woman in a hooded sweatshirt move through the restaurant and go back to the stairs that led down to the lower levels. "My wife and I got this footage while we were there eating lunch."

"Holy shit!" Fitz said as Kenyon froze the frame, capturing a fraction of a second where the side of Zoë's face could be seen.

"Maybe she's headed down to that secret level," Kenyon added.

"What secret level?"

"It seems that Ray Senior had a small subterranean annex built in the late seventies when the new subway leg was installed."

"How did you guys find out about this?"

"We've got our sources, Captain."

"So this is adjacent to the bathrooms in the basement?"

"Below them…the bureau has been trying to get into that room for twenty years."

"I'm sorry Joel, but you're going to have to excuse me."

"Okay…?" Kenyon replied completely puzzled as Fitz slipped back out into the crowd, digging into his pocket for his alternate cell phone. Without even looking at it he hit the *send* button and put it to his ear.

"The party you are trying to reach is unavailable. Please leave a message. Beeeeep!"

"Roman, call me as soon as you get this. I can't tell you where this came from but we know Zoë was at Evangeline's on Wednesday. She was last seen heading down to the lower levels."

* * *

As the dream progressed, Roman held his daughter for the first time. She was so small, an attribute complicated by the fact that she was two weeks early. She was healthy though, and for a brief second that made him smile.

"Did you two talk about a name?" Maria asked.

"Theodore if it was a boy. Evangeline for a girl."

"Middle name?"

"No... just Evangeline."

"Evangeline Sabarese. Very pretty," the nurse said as she typed out the hospital birth certificate.

Roman continued to hold her. He was completely transfixed by what he saw. As he started to fall deeper into that memory, a phone conversation filled his sleeping head.

"Melanie..." the dreamer said with a lumbering voice.

"Roman? What is it? Is everything alright?"

"I need for you to come over to Brooklyn Methodist as soon as you can."

"What is it?"

"I'll explain when you get here."

Roman looked at his daughter for what was to be the last time. As Melanie Greene walked down the long hall with her new baby, Fitz and Maria exchanged a complicit look of agreement. Roman stood and simply watched in silence as his baby's new mother walked further away with every step. She held Evangeline tight. And tucked away in her purse was a new, updated birth certificate listing Melanie as the mother, typed out by nurse Maria Gomez, who also like the name Zoë...Zoë Greene.

* * *

"Captain, it's starting," one of the uniformed officers announced.

Fitz walked back out into the street where a solid sea of people had started to yell in unison, chanting the age old New Year's countdown. The ball, a custom made version for this special year, started to fall slowly as the crowd counted backwards.

7 – 6 – 5 – 4 – 3 – 2 – 1

"HAPPY NEW YEAR!" they yelled in an alcohol-assisted unison. Fitz looked up with a smile as a half-inebriated woman dressed in micro shorts and a bikini top confronted him with a wet kiss on the lips.

"Well then…hello!" he remarked with an even bigger smile, picking up his alternate cell phone again, trying to call Roman.

* * *

The dream moved through time and space as though an urgent message from Roman's subconscious was burning a path to his daily mind. It was yesterday and he was sitting in the restaurant's kitchen, listening to the simple answers Devon the dishwasher had been giving to Fitz.

"Ghosts are in the dungeon. Zoë's a ghost," Devon had said. The words haunted him in his sleep. And then, as though his dream was a processor and his mind a hard drive, another thought appeared, that of Devon asking for his keys because the one for the sub-basement was missing. It all made sense. Now all Roman had to do was wake up.

Chapter 41

January 1st, 2000

The city was quiet as Roman drew open his drapes, letting a flood of light into his dark apartment. While he was in the habit of forgetting most of his dreams, Roman remembered every inch of the reel that played through his mind the previous night, especially the part where Devon had made the statement about Zoë being a ghost in the dungeon.

His cell phone sat on the couch. On its face, a red blinking light indicated that he had missed at least one call. Almost immediately he dialed his voicemail number, entered his pass code and waited.

"Roman, call me as soon as you get this. I can't tell you where this came from but we know Zoë was at Evangeline's on Wednesday. She was last seen heading down to the lower levels."

Three minutes later Roman pulled his pickup out of the garage and made a quick left onto the southbound lane of Park Avenue. The streets were quiet and still which was a stark contrast to the way they looked just a few hours before. Manhattan had expended its last bit of energy and the city that never slept was now taking a much-deserved nap. As the sun rose through the towering buildings, the street was covered with a collage of paper stretching from sidewalk to sidewalk, the fallout of the biggest party on the planet.

Roman sped faster as he ran two lights in a row and rounded the split in Park Avenue that encircled the MetLife Building. *How could I have been so stupid? She was right there all along,* he thought to himself, punishing the ideas in his mind from the days before. *Poor Devon!* They had written off his ramblings as just that, ramblings, when all along, his simple words held the clue.

As he pulled into the alley behind the restaurant, he couldn't get out of the truck fast enough. He fumbled for his keys, unlocking the deadbolts and single crossbar at the back door. Once inside he made a beeline for the women's bathroom, bursting through the door. His heart started to beat faster as he thumbed through more keys before realizing that they weren't necessary. The door that led below to the sub-basement was unlocked. The light past there was poor so he negotiated each step with caution, making it to the bottom. As he stepped off the last few stairs to the floor, his feet splashed into thirty inches of acrid seawater that rose up past his knees. Roman sloshed over to the freezer like an anxious child wading through the water at the beach. His heart was now pounding through his shirt as he grabbed the dysfunctional handle to the antique icebox. The door swung open and the light from the room flashed on Zoë who was sitting atop the cradle, shivering in the darkness and squinting while she adjusted to the sudden change in light.

* * *

Fitz awoke with a stiff back and neck. It was the byproduct of the short night he spent on a military style cot that had been se up in the temporary police command center at Times Square. As he sat up, a sharp pain shot through his spine like a lightning bolt.

"You okay?" one of the detectives asked, noticing the grimace on his face.

"Jesus…thanks, but yeah. Do I have cancer written on my forehead? What time is it anyway?" Fitz asked.

"07:10 AM. First morning of the new millennium and we're all still here."

"Shit!" he said, reaching for the jacket that concealed his alternate cell phone. "I'll be back in a bit."

"But…the mayor's office is cooking us breakfast."

"Save me a plate, okay?"

"Got it Chief."

Fitz bolted out of the center and onto the street. Times Square looked like a bomb had been detonated…a paper bomb. The street was void of people and cluttered with the overwhelming residue of confetti, plastic and discarded food. In some places the debris was several inches thick. Fitz donned a wrinkled jacket over his half buttoned uniform as he ran his fingers through his gray hair and dialed Roman's number with his free hand.

* * *

Across town and sitting on the front seat of Roman Sabarese's truck, his cell phone rang without being answered. It continued through ten cycles before going to voicemail. Outside the truck, a man wearing a khaki safari vest and a camera around his neck walked into the alley. As he passed the vehicle's driver side window, he spotted the ringing phone. He cupped his hands over the truck's glass to shield the light so he could look inside before slipping into the shadows of the alley.

* * *

Back at the command center, Fitz slid into the seat of his gray, unmarked Crown Victoria police car, turned the ignition and within seconds was squealing out of the specially reserved police parking area with a trail of loose paper and debris in his wake.

Park Avenue was almost empty. It was an eerie sight for someone who had spent his life in bumper-to-bumper traffic on the same streets. Still, the intermittent traffic signals seemed to flash from green to amber to red on his account. Out of frustration he ignited the red and blue flashing strobes that were concealed behind the car's windshield. With an occasional yelp from the siren, he sliced through each intersection without looking back.

Fitz, like most cops, had developed a finely tuned extra-sense that told him when something was out of place. Now his mental alarms were going off as he stomped on the car's gas pedal. The V-eight engine hummed under the hood as his speed approached seventy miles per hour. A few more yelps of the siren echoed from the tall buildings as the car squealed through more paper and debris, rounding the intersection at Duane Street as he drove south on Greenwich Street towards Evangeline's.

* * *

Zoë was cold, shivering, and suffering from the early stages o hypothermia. The two looked at each other without saying a wor before Roman picked her up in his arms and walked through th knee-deep water as they made their way out of the restaurant' bottom level. It was the first time that he had held her weight sinc her day of birth. Zoë held her father's arms as tight as she could as h climbed the tall, steep two flights of stairs. She looked up at his fac as he struggled with every step. His shoes were wet and sloshed as he walked. She looked at him differently now. Still so many questions and yet now, so many more answers. When they made it to the top of the last set of steps, she dropped down and stood, trying to keep her balance. Her legs felt awkward from the lack of use and her stance lacked confidence. Roman leaned over again and picked her up, scooping her tighter this time with both arms. As they exited the back door, Zoë squinted again as her pupils adjusted to the much brighter sunlight. The air, in contrast to what she had just breathed, was as fresh as a breeze from a North Carolina mountaintop. From there it was a short distance to the passenger door of Roman's truck. Once seated, she looked over at him and for the first time since her ordeal had begun, she felt safe. As Roman made his way to the driver's side, he caught a glimpse of a shadow moving towards him from behind the dumpster.

"Not you again," he said, thinking it was the paparazzi photographer he had run off a few days before. As the man came into the light he stopped and faced Roman squarely. It was Sully, Big John Ciasuli's henchman, and he was wearing a khaki safari vest and had a camera draped from his neck.

"I'm sorry Roman," the man said, pulling a .45 pistol from his vest. Roman stopped in disbelief as Sully, the photog turned shooter, fired three rounds into his chest. Inside the truck Zoë's scream was muffled by the cabin insulation. Time seemed to freeze as she watched the shooter raise his gun and point it in her direction. All she could hear was the ringing in her own ears, the result of the loud percussion created by the three shots.

"No...please..." she cried.

Then, without warning, the sound of screeching tires filled the end of the alley as Fitz skidded to a stop. Sully looked away for a second and fired in Fitz's direction as Zoë grabbed the door latch and rolled out of the passenger side door onto the cold snow-covered pavement below. The round from the gun entered the windshield of the detective's car, grazing him on the right side of his forehead. Immediately, blood started to trickle down his face. Sully looked back in Zoë's direction just in time to see her head exit the opposite side of the truck as he fired a desperate shot in her direction, striking the vehicle's back window. The glass shattered into a thousand diamond-like pieces.

"Freeze! Drop your gun!" Fitz yelled as he stood next to his car, shielding himself behind the open driver's side door. Sully turned towards him and with a fluid motion his gun soon followed, aiming towards the prepared policeman.

Breathe, stance, aim and squeeze, Fitz thought as he entered his familiar quiet place and fired a quick double round in the man's direction. Both slugs raced the length of the alley with the first one striking Sully's chest a few inches left of center. The second round penetrated him squarely through his forehead, blowing out the back of his skull. The shock rocked the shooter backwards as he fell to the dirty snow below.

Fitz held his stance as he yelled towards the truck. "Come out slowly," he watched as two shaking hands rose up past the bed of the truck. As Zoë stood, Fitz lowered his gun with a sigh of relief.

"Are you hurt?"

"No…please help him!" she cried, pointing towards Roman as Fitz looked over seeing the man lying on the ground with a blood stained shirt that was draining into the snow.

"Car 112…shots fired…men down. The alley behind 323 Greenwich Street. Send EMU and backup!" Fitz barked into his portable radio as the dispatcher squawked back a hasty reply. "Are you sure you're okay?" he asked as he got closer to Zoë.

"I'm alright. Please…" she replied pointing to Roman.

Fitz moved towards him. He was trying to breathe through the froth of bright red blood that was forming at his mouth as Fitz got down on a knee and put his heavy police jacket over him.

"Hang in there man. Help's on the way."

"Please help! He's my father!" Zoë cried.

"Yes, he is Zoë," Fitz said.

"Who are you?"

"A friend."

"Please help us."

"Where's that EMU?" Fitz barked again into the mic of his handheld radio.

"Two minutes 112," the dispatcher replied as the sound of approaching sirens filled the surrounding streets.

"Hold his head. Here…keep it straight. This will make it easier for him to breathe," he instructed as Zoë cupped her hands around his ears. She looked down at him as his eyes opened and he gurgled more blood as he tried to talk.

"I love you," she said with bloodshot, tear-filled eyes as Fitz looked over at Sully who was cold, still and well-departed. Roman's eyes opened wide as he looked into her face. Without words the two connected for the last time as his blood drenched breath flowed from his lungs and he too became still. Zoë lowered her head, touching her forehead to his.

Two EMU paramedics ran up to Fitz who sat down in the snow.

"Captain! Are you alright?" one asked as the other put a piece of gauze against his bleeding head.

"Him?" the other medic asked, pointing towards Roman. Fitz shook his head *no*.

As the men tended to his wound and the alley filled with scores of uniformed officers, he just stared at Zoë who stayed frozen in place with her forehead against his. Her crying stopped as she took the time to absorb what few moments she would have left with her father.

Epilogue

Deep inside the cold halls of the Danbury Federal Correctional Institution, Big John Ciasuli sat in the metal chair and waited. A buzzer alarmed as the clink of bars sounded and the heavy steel door slid open on its tracks. Ray Senior entered the family room wearing his usual attire, dark blue pants and a light blue work shirt with his name and inmate number affixed to the right breast pocket.

"I hear it's done," Senior said.

"It is," Big John replied.

"It makes me sad, but it had to happen this way."

"If you say so."

"I know you two were close," he said as Big John stared back at him."I need you to try to get the money from the accounts he set up in Dubai and secure them in Grand Cayman," Senior instructed.

"I can't."

"What do you mean you can't?"

"Roman set up a failsafe amendment to the portfolio."

"What?"

"Upon his death, all the money goes to one beneficiary."

"Will I regret asking who that might be?"

"Probably."

"So what do we do?"

"I don't know what you're gonna do, but I've got a my own business to run."

"You can't be serious. I always considered you to be a loyal captain."

"And I was, but this thing, this last thing was the end of the line for me. I'm done. I paid my fee, albeit to Roman, but it's paid. You left him in charge. You made that decision. I'm on my own."

"You traitor!"

"You killed your own son. You disgust me. All that this thing of ours has stood for after all these years…it has always been about family," Big John announced with a dominant tone. "I'll say it again, I'm done, and for what it's worth, you ever mess with that kid again and you'll have to answer to me. Got it?"

And with that Big John stood and walked over to the exit where he hit a red button on the wall. A buzzer sounded inside the guard's office and a steel door rolled open as the former captain turned to look back at Ray Senior one last time.

* * *

It had been a year since Roman's death and Evangeline's was open for a special exclusive New Year's Eve party. "The *real* birth of the millennium," as Zoë called it. And while it lacked the fanfare of the year before, she made sure that everyone attending knew that this was an equally special occasion. It was, however, more about reflection than celebration.

The headlines that morning told the bigger story.

Mob Boss Dead at 82

Imprisoned underworld crime boss Roman Sabarese Senior was found dead in his cell at Danbury Federal Correctional Institution early yesterday morning. The initial cause has been reported as an apparent stroke, although a medical examiner has not yet made an official determination.

It was bittersweet for her. Ray Sabarese Senior was, after all, her grandfather despite the fact that he did orchestrate the killing of both her parents and attempt to murder her while she was still in her mother's womb. The last of the baggage that had adversely affected her life was gone though, and now she could focus on the bright future that was ahead. *This next year was going to be huge,* she imagined.

As for the party, *real* millennium or not, there were so many reasons to pay tribute. For one, Zoë was back in town after shooting the lead in an action film that would be distributed worldwide and grace the silver screens of every major market in the industry. The project had her shooting scenes all throughout Europe and, while she enjoyed the travel, it was good to be home. She had also been given the opportunity to direct her first feature.

As far as the restaurant was concerned, it had enjoyed a record year under the watchful eye of Nello, who was celebrating with Devon at his side. Both wore matching aprons with Evangeline's embroidered in gold letters across the breast. It was part of a new and updated look for the restaurant, one that she had implemented on her own as a way of moving on. And while many raved at the changes, few noticed when the Italian Consulate revoked the eatery's status as an official diplomatic annex. Across the street from Evangeline's and on the fourth floor where the DSS "security" detail had once assembled with its cameras and telescopes, a bright red *For Rent* sign was seen hanging in the window.

While Zoë had proved her flexibility by being able to take on any role Hollywood put in her path, the role she felt the most comfortable in was that of the restaurant's hostess. It gave her an enormous amount of pleasure to stand behind the podium and welcome her guests, especially on this night when she could be of service to so many who had been of service to her.

After greeting a dozen or so couples, guests she had handpicked, her most honored patrons approached the podium. Captain Stanley Fitzgerald and his date, nurse Maria Gomez, the two people she had learned that were actually her godparents and angels having saved her not once, but twice. She enjoyed talking to them the previous year, especially Maria who gave such vivid accounts of her mother Bettina. After time she left the podium to join her guardians where a reoccurring debate continued between Zoë and Fitz.

"All the predictions, the great disasters at the beginning of the new millennium, you're saying we didn't dodge the bullet? So, you're saying that if these prognosticators are correct, we will see a cataclysmic event in 2001?" Fitz reasoned.

"It's anyone's guess. We will just have to wait and see," Zoë replied.

"I think I like my calculation better. I don't know if I can take another year like the last. And, I still don't see how we were all a year off," he remarked, having survived a long year of chemotherapy. His reward, and another cause for celebration, had come a few weeks before in the form of an oncology report that stated he was in full remission.

"You see Fritz, if you are working ten hours, your shift doesn't end at the beginning of the tenth hour. Does it?"

"No, but..."

"You have to include the last year. By celebrating the end of the millennium this last year, well…it shortchanged us by a whole 365 days."

"So why did everyone make such a big deal last year?"

"It's all about perception, and on certain occasions, occasions that effect us all, perception, unfortunately, becomes reality."

"So you didn't really miss the big new year, did you?" Maria suggested.

"No ma'am. And I get to spend it with *most* of the people with whom I hold dear to my heart. I only wish Roman were also with us," Zoë replied as she looked over at Melanie. Her mother looked back at her with a proud smile that stretched across her face. They were all seated together at their own private table, the owner's table, table 21.

The End.